POTIONS, POISONS, AND PERIL

Deepwood Witches Mysteries
Book One

Shéa MacLeod

The characters and events portrayed in this book are fictitious. Any similarity to real persons, living or dead is coincidental and not intended by the author.

Potions, Poisons, and Peril
Text copyright © 2019 Shéa MacLeod
All rights reserved.

Printed in the United States of America.

Cover design by Mariah Sinclair/mariahsinclair.com
Editing by Theo Fenraven
Formatted with D2D

Still for Nora

Because shenanigans.

CHAPTER
ONE

A teaspoon of sugar for sweetness to the day. A dollop of cream for spirituality. Stir counterclockwise.

It was the same tea ritual Emory Chastain had used every morning for as long as she could remember. A way to start the day out right. To embrace the magic of living.

Sunlight streamed through the kitchen window, bathing her in a golden glow and sending colors from the Victorian stained-glass dancing over the walls.

She tilted her head back, smiling when her chinchilla, Fred, bounced onto the counter, then up to her shoulder, curling sleepily into her hair. Chinchillas were a nocturnal sort, but Fred liked to stick close, even during daylight hours.

"May the heat of the sun, glow of moon, glory of fire, swiftness of wind, strength of water, and endurance of earth guide and protect me this day. As I will, so mote it be."

She caught the time out of the corner of her eye. If she didn't hurry, she wouldn't have time for donuts. Draining her tea, she snagged her phone and keys off the counter and strode for the front door, long cotton skirt swishing around her legs.

There was enough time, however, to stop and bury her face in a rose. There was always time to smell the roses. They hung heavy over the rusted wrought iron fence, waving slightly in the faint breeze.

The blue Victorian—and its garden and fence—was still in need of work with its door faded to a tomato red and the broken step up to the porch, but it was all hers. Her perfect sanctuary.

Popping her earbuds in, she cranked up Diana Ross's "I'm Coming Out" as she marched down the sidewalk toward the donut shop, mindful of Fred's slight weight on her shoulder. The energy of the song and the day buzzed through her, and she smiled at everyone she passed, from her grumpy neighbor walking his elderly, incontinent dachshund to the gaggle of yoga moms sipping chai lattes outside the bakery.

Deepwood was one of those small towns that popped up in Hallmark Channel movies and romance novels. Cute, quaint, large enough to have multiple coffee shops and baked goods stores but small enough to feel cozy and inviting.

Main Street—how boring a name could you get? —stretched for several blocks and was essentially the main drag where everyone and everything congregated. Technically the center of "downtown" was four blocks over, near the town hall, but no one paid that any mind. Main Street was where it was at, including Emory's shop, Healing Herbs.

Emory veered into what would have been a plain box of a building if it wasn't painted bubblegum pink and popped out her earbuds, leaving Diana behind. Built in the '40s, it had been one of those squat stucco numbers with zero personality that had served as a perfect office building until Virgil Zante had taken over and turned it into Pink Lady Donuts. Now it was shockingly cheerful and very, very pink. No one knew who the pink lady was, and no one had ever bothered to ask. It was more fun to speculate, Emory supposed. Some said it was Virgil's mother, or perhaps a lost love. Still others thought it was Virgil himself.

Emory didn't much care either way. Virgil made the best donuts in the history of donuts. She ought to know. She'd eaten enough of them.

Virgil glanced up from restocking the pastry case, a smile on his pink face. The smile grew wider when he saw it was Emory. "My lady! Your usual is ready." He set down the half empty tray of crullers and handed her a pink box. "Hello, Fred."

Fred popped his head out long enough to take an unsalted almond from Virgil.

Emory and Virgil had a standing agreement. Every morning he had a dozen donuts ready for her. Half of them were old favorites, like maple bars and blueberry cake. The other half were experiments: mango-chutney filled, peanut butter and banana fritters, cardamom with white chocolate drizzle, CBD infused tomato basil. In return for feedback on his unusual creations, she got a steep discount.

Virgil and Fred had a different understanding. Virgil offered Fred treats, and Fred accepted them.

"Thanks, Virgil! Sorry, no time to chat. Blessed be!"

He laughed as she popped in her earbuds. "Blessed be, Emory."

That was the thing about Deepwood. It wasn't just a quaint, charming town. It was a town of witches. Mostly. Oh, there were mundanes—non-magical people. And supernatural types such as djinn and fairies and the occasional vampire, but mostly it was witches. In Virgil's case, he was Wiccan rather than a true witch, although Emory could have sworn he worked pure magic in the kitchen.

Emory's shop was smack in the middle of Main Street, halfway from the grocery store at one end and the library at the other. It was in a brick-fronted building with wide windows and a bright green awning. She'd hand-lettered the open/closed sign herself, adding a spell to it that would either encourage visitors or repel intruders, depending on which side was facing out.

Inside, she set the donut box on the register counter before scooping Fred off her shoulder and tucking him into the giant Victorian birdcage behind the counter. It served as his home away from home. Next she turned on the overhead lights and switched the sign to Open. She was already five minutes late.

Selecting a bundle of dried rosemary, she lit it, then slowly walked the perimeter of the shop, chanting low as the fragrant smoke cleansed the shop of anything negative that might have gathered overnight.

Negativity that has gathered in this place,
I banish you with my light and my grace.
You have no power and no hold here,
And of you I have no fear.
Begone forever away from me.
As I will so mote it be."

She blew out the embers and returned the bundle to its place beneath the counter. Then she happily flipped open the lid on the donut box and selected one of Virgil's latest creations. He'd written on it in icing *lime and jalapeno.*

"Well, that ought to be interesting."

Before she could take a bite, the door burst open and a woman strode in. "I need a love potion."

The woman glared at Emory belligerently, lower jaw thrust forward. Her skinny body was swathed in a massive fake fur coat, despite the warmth of an early summer morning, and her mousy brown hair was scraped into a tight bun on top of her head. Her muddy eyes snapped in anger, as if Emory had somehow personally affronted her.

She was used to working with challenging customers. She gave the woman a placating smile as she reluctantly returned her donut to the box, inhaled through her nose, and mentally repeated, *Don't turn the customer into a frog. Don't turn the customer into a frog.*

Fred chittered in his birdcage as if to say, *Go ahead. Turn her into a frog and let me bite her.*

She ducked her head to hide a smile. Not that she could turn the woman into a frog. Her magic didn't run that way, though there were some days that would come in real handy.

She waved a quieting hand at Fred as she surreptitiously studied the woman's aura. It was heavily tinged with poisonous green. Jealousy, and a lot of it. No way was she handing this woman anything with power.

"I'm sorry, we don't carry love potions," Emory lied. She picked up a small brown bottle. "I have a nice herbal tincture for relaxation and stress relief." It wasn't the first time she'd been asked for a love potion, but one had to be cautious when dealing with magical elixirs. Emory only gave true magic to those in real need.

"I don't need relaxation," the customer snapped, her aura flaring an angry red. "I need a love potion. I was told you do that kind of thing."

She carefully blanked her face. "Do what kind of thing?" Deepwood might be a witchy town filled with practitioners of the magical arts, but that didn't mean they went around blabbing to strangers. And this woman was definitely a stranger.

The woman let out a huff of annoyance and edged a little closer. She caught a whiff of dusty roses and mothballs. "Magic."

Emory gave a light laugh, noticing the thick brown smudge along the woman's aura. Greed. "I can't help you."

"That's not what I hear." The woman edged forward, shrewd eyes watching Emory like a hawk.

Every molecule in her body was immediately on high alert. Fred's chittering grew more aggravated. "I don't know what you mean. This is a simple herb shop. Clearly, whoever told you otherwise was mistaken."

The woman snorted. "Don't play coy with me," she snapped. "I am sick of playing second fiddle. I want my man to leave his cow of a wife and marry me. So give me that love potion. Now!"

She was right up in Emory's personal space. Unease shivered through her. She didn't have much in the way of offensive spells, and there was no way she was giving this woman a love potion so she could steal another woman's husband. She sent out a mental call for help.

"Listen, witch," the woman in the fur coat hissed. She grabbed Emory's arm, her fingernails digging into pale flesh like claws. "I want that love potion, and I want it now."

Fred bounced in his cage, angry chitters growing louder by the second. Emory yanked, but the nails dug in, sending pain shooting up her arm. She tried not to wince, but her mouth was dry with fear. This woman might be a mundane, but extreme avarice had made her strong and crazy.

"Give it to me," the woman screeched, her face twisted into a caricature, "or else."

"Or else what?" someone boomed from the doorway.

Emory and the woman stared, startled. Two women stood there like the Furies reborn, arms akimbo, faces wreathed in righteous anger. Emory almost wilted in relief at the sight of them.

"Let. Her. Go." The blonde strode forward, her eyes pools of black ink, a threat in every word. Her pale skin glowed moon bright, and her cheeks flushed pink with determination.

The other woman kept pace beside her, curly black-brown hair floating in a gust of wind no one else could feel. Her eyes had turned silver, starkly bright against her dark skin.

Fred bounced to the front of his cage, a ball of dark gray fur with a whipping tail and sharp teeth. He let out an enraged screech, pressing tiny paws against the bars.

The woman in the fur coat stumbled back, hands held up as if to ward everyone off.

"I didn't mean to cause no trouble," the customer all but whimpered, the fight gushing out of her. "I won't bother you no more." Gone was the haughty tone and elegant inflection. Sweat beaded her brow and upper lip.

"See that you don't," Emory snapped, cradling her injured arm. "Go now and don't return. I banish thee. As I will so mote it be."

The woman paled, then whirled, the fur coat fanning dramatically behind her, and scurried out the door, slamming it behind her so hard, the windowpane next to it rattled ominously.

Emory heaved a sigh of relief, she leaned down and scooped Fred out of his cage, rubbing her chin over his impossibly soft fur to calm both of them. "Thanks, ladies. She was, uh, a little scary."

The blonde rushed forward and gave Emory a quick hug. Her eyes had bled from black back to their natural blue, which matched the blue of her Wonder Woman T-shirt. "Are you okay?"

"I'm fine, Lene," she assured her best friend. "She just creeped me out. Gave me a nice set of claw marks as a memento, too." Emory showed them the bloody furrows raked across her skin, like blood on snow.

Lene—"Lehnah not Lenny"—Davenport made a distressed sound. "I'll get the med kit." She hurried to the back room, her flip-flops slapping against the wood floor with little sploging sounds.

"What did that nasty woman want, anyway?" the other witch, Veri, asked. Her eyes had returned to a soft, warm brown that complimented her rich, brown skin.

Emory popped open Fred's house. She urged him inside, handed him a raisin, then latched the door. He nibbled on his treat in ecstasy, the earlier drama forgotten. "She said she wanted a love potion. Claimed someone told her I carried them."

Veri snorted, fluffing out the skirt of her tangerine '50s style dress. "Please. That woman was full of crazy. Did you see the greed in her aura? No way anyone we know would send her our way."

Veri was right. The world at large knew nothing about the truth of Deepwood. The town kept their secrets well hidden.

"She was probably just guessing," Lene said, returning from the storeroom with an old sewing basket. It had belonged to Emory's grandmother, except Emory didn't sew, so she'd converted it into a medical kit. "Word gets around, you know. Probably heard a rumor and thought she'd give it a try. Claimed someone had told her about you so you'd be more willing to give up the goods."

"True," Veri said thoughtfully as Lene pushed Emory into a chair and rummaged in the med kit. "Decided to take a gamble. Lost big time."

"Thanks for rescuing me, though I was hoping to get her out of here without giving away the fact that we can do magic. Denial is always the best way to go when it comes to outsiders." It was essential to keep things low key. Emory did not want the world at large knowing that not only was magic real, so were witches. The last thing they needed was another installment of the Salem Witch Trials, only this time in Oregon instead of Massachusetts.

"Hey, what are friends for?" Veri said with a shrug. "Listen, everything under control here? Because I left the shop unmanned." Veri was not only her friend and a fellow coven member, she also owned the lingerie store next door to Emory's shop, in the other half of the building.

Emory waved her off and closed her eyes as Lene silently cleaned and bandaged her arm. She pinched the bridge of her nose. A headache lurked behind her eyes. Maybe she needed a dose of one of her tinctures.

"Sorry about spilling the beans," Lene said as she tucked the supplies back in the sewing basket. "It was just awful seeing that woman attacking you like that, and you not using any magic or anything."

"Don't worry about it." Emory squeezed her hand. "It'll be fine. What's one gold digger wanting a stupid love potion, anyway?" But deep down Emory had a feeling of foreboding. Not necessarily about the woman, but something was coming. She cleared her throat. "Don't you have something to do other than fuss over me?"

Lene shook her head, her blonde mane bouncing dramatically. "The bookstore was completely empty when you called. I activated a ward before I left so no one will come in."

Lene owned the town's only bookstore, Second Sight Books. It was tucked into an old cottage next to Veri and Emory's building. Lene carried mostly used books, and the store was frequently busy. She also did a thriving online business, locating rare, magical texts for out-of-town witches.

The bell jangled above the shop door, and Emory glanced up, half expecting the love potion lady to reappear. But it was a young woman wearing an enormous pair of hot pink sunglasses and a brown pageboy that was obviously a wig. She glanced around nervously before approaching the counter.

She cleared her throat. "Emory Chastain?"

She felt a momentary flutter of trepidation. "That's me."

"My name is"—she hesitated—"Julia. I live out near the funeral home." She probably meant Deepwood Mortuary on the bluff overlooking the Willamette River. Nice neighborhood. "Um, I read about your shop online. How you had that love magic event awhile back."

Emory and Lene exchanged glances as Emory rose to her feet. "That was a popular event. I still have some of the products, if you're interested."

Julia swallowed. "N-no thanks. That's not what I'm here for."

Emory gave Lene a look and, with a nod, Lene faded into the background, though she didn't stray far, despite having a shop to run. After the incident with the love potion lady, she wasn't about to leave Emory alone.

Emory waved her new client to the small alcove in the corner, where two comfortable chairs were placed around a small, low table. It was the perfect spot for sipping tea or reading tarot cards. "Would you like to sit?"

Julia shook her head. "I don't have much time."

"Very well. How may I help you?" She kept her voice quiet and even. She had a feeling her newest customer was the type who spooked easily.

Julia slid her glasses off. Emory tried not to wince. The skin around the young woman's left eye was swollen and purple. Somebody had belted her good. Her palms itched with the need to punch whoever it was in some place a lot more sensitive than an eye.

"Who did that?" Emory couldn't help asking the question, though it was invasive.

"My husband." Julia's voice was so soft, Emory could barely hear her.

"Does he do that often?"

Julia tilted her chin up a little, and Emory admired her struggle to be strong. Leaving abusive jerks could be difficult, if not impossible, for some. It was also dangerous and very brave.

"Yes."

She swallowed her outrage and the strong language that rose to her tongue. She had to remain calm if she was going to help her. "What do you need me to do?" Hopefully the woman wouldn't ask her to put a curse on him. Although she was sorely tempted, she didn't want it bouncing back on her threefold. There were rules when it came to magic. Whatever you put out in the universe was what you got back in spades. Including bad juju.

Julia cleared her throat and replaced her glasses. "Hide me."

Emory smiled. "Now that I can do."

Her gold gladiator sandals slapped lightly against the wood floor as she strode to a nearby display table. The footwear was her concession to working with the public, although she hated anything on her feet. It blocked her connection to Mother Earth. She missed the constant ebb and flow of energy between her and the planet, but the mundane world had its demands.

She grabbed a bar of soap from a table and a bottle of lotion from the glass shelves and returned to her client. "Take these," she said, handing Julia the items.

The young woman stared at the lotion and soap. "Skin care products?" She frowned. "That's not going to hide me from my husband."

"You came here for my help, yes?"

She nodded. Emory couldn't see much of her eyes behind the glasses. *Does she have any idea what I can do?*

"Then believe those bath products aren't ordinary."

"Okay." Julia's voice was shaky. "What do I do?"

"You have somewhere to stay? Somewhere your husband doesn't know about?"

"Yes, I—"

"Don't tell me," she said, holding up her hand. "It's better if I don't know. Just in case."

"All right."

"The minute you get to where you're staying, take a shower and wash with that soap. While you do, picture in your mind walking past your husband on the street and him not even noticing you. Then do the same with the lotion when you get out of the shower. Imagine you're slathering on an invisibility barrier. He looks at you, but he doesn't see you. Got it?"

"Got it. But how is that going to work?"

"The mind is a powerful thing, Julia. This will work, I promise. But it's only temporary. Three or four days at most, so you need to get out of town as soon as possible." She walked over to the counter, opened a drawer, took out a business card, and handed it to Julia.

"Norma's Diner?" Julia asked, glancing at the card.

"They've got really good pie. Someone watched *Twin Peaks* one time too many. I suggest visiting soon. Go today if you can. Tomorrow at the latest. Speak to the waitress there."

"Which one?"

Emory smiled. "There's only one. Edwina." Edwina was also the owner. "Tell her you need to disappear. She'll handle the rest."

"Can I trust her?"

Emory gave her a measured look. "Can you trust anyone?"

Julia sighed. "Good point. Thanks for... this. How much do I owe you?"

"One day, when you're safe, pay it forward. Good luck."

Julia nodded and hurried to the door, her sneakers squeaking on the polished wood. The bell jangled as she slipped out. Emory heaved a sigh. A witch's work was never done.

Potions, Poisons and Peril

CHAPTER TWO

Over the years, Deepwood had become a destination for antique shoppers as Main Street turned into what many referred to as "antiques row." Weekends, the town was packed with visitors from the big city, hunting for good deals. These days, there were fewer antique shops and more cafes and coffee shops, not to mention plenty of pot shops. It was the perfect place for a store that sold herbs and spices, and tinctures and magical potions masquerading as ordinary skin care products.

Some of the items Emory carried, she made herself, bespelling them in her kitchen. Others were made by local witches and imbued with their powers. Still others were brought in from mundane manufacturers and left as-is or touched with a bit of spellwork in her back room. Most of the stuff for sale had only the merest touch of magic. The truly strong stuff was kept under lock and key, away from the general public. Only special customers got those.

"Hottie alert."

Lene beckoned wildly at the shop window. Emory's breath caught at the sight of the man getting out of a black jeep. "Holy moly."

"I know, right?" Lene was trying to hide behind the display of herbal teas, but her ample backside, clad in faded blue jeans, stuck out like the proverbial sore thumb. Emory probably would have laughed if her attention hadn't been on the gorgeous man outside.

He was tall, at least six feet but probably more, with one of those perfectly sculpted bodies that put Michelangelo's David to shame. Silky smooth skin the color of rich brown clay made her hands itch to stroke it, even from a distance. He turned his back to the shop to put money in the parking meter, and she bit her lip so hard, it nearly split open. He had a backside you could bounce a quarter off.

Forget that. You could bounce a freaking fifty-cent piece off that butt. She zinged with instant attraction to a stranger. Goddess above, she was in trouble.

"Would you get away from the window?" she hissed, as though the guy outside might hear. "He might see you, plus you look like an idiot."

"I'm waiting for him to turn around," Lene snapped back, tucking a blonde curl behind her ear. Her pale skin had a suspicious shimmer to it Emory hadn't noticed earlier. No doubt she'd been sampling Veronique's glitter lotions again. "I want to get a good look at his face and see if it matches the rest of him."

Emory rolled her eyes. "Bet it doesn't." Just because he had a nice backside didn't mean he had a nice face. Or personality. She'd had plenty of awful dates in her lifetime that bore that out.

Like the time she'd gone out with a fairy halfling. He'd spent the entire time flirting with the waitress. Or the djinn who'd snuck out after ordering every expensive entrée on the meal and left her to pay for it all. Both of them had been exceedingly handsome. At least on the outside.

The hottie suddenly turned around, catching Lene gaping at him through the window. She gave him a little finger wave, which he good-naturedly returned, along with a wry smile loaded with dimples. *Points to him.* Either he was used to having crazy women stare at him from shop windows, or he was just a good sport. One thing was for certain: his face definitely matched the rest of him. She was pretty sure you could cut rock with those cheekbones, and the thick lashes framing slightly almond-shaped bedroom eyes the color of rich umber would make any woman weep with envy.

As he disappeared from view, Lene let out a squeal. "Ohmylanta! He's going next door."

"I guess another one bites the dust," Emory said. Ignoring the pang of disappointment, she turned her attention back to the inventory sheet. The soy candles and black cohosh were not going to count themselves.

"What do you mean?" Lene was still staring out the window as if trying to catch the very last glimpse of the hottie.

"You know what's next door."

"Veri's shop, Dangerous Curves," she answered immediately. "So?"

"Only married men or men with girlfriends go there."

"Don't be silly. He could be single. You don't know. Maybe he's shopping for his mother. Or his sister."

"Now who's being silly?" She laughed. "Men do not buy gifts for their relatives at Dangerous Curves." Unless they wanted to give those relatives heart attacks. "Veri would be the first to tell you that."

"I'm going to wait until he comes out, then I'll go ask Veronique."

"You do that. In the meantime, don't you have your own shop to run."

"Aye, Captain. That I do." Lene gave her a snappy salute and marched out the door to her bookstore.

Emory stared out the window for a minute, her mind wandering. Six months ago, Veronique Laveau had shown up out of nowhere and opened Dangerous Curves next to Emory's herb shop. It had changed her life.

At first, she'd worried a plus-sized lingerie shop might be bad for business. In her admittedly meager experience, such places, while few and far between, were usually tacky, trashy, and full of cheap panties and ill-fitting bras. Not Dangerous Curves. Veronique believed women of all sizes had the right to wear beautiful things that fit properly and gave the right amount of support. Her sexy, slinky undergarments found their way into Emory's lingerie drawer at an alarming rate. Despite the damage to her bank account, and having no one to show them off to, Emory firmly believed they were worth every penny. It was amazing what a pair of gorgeous, matching, perfectly fitting underthings could do for a woman's confidence.

But it wasn't just Emory's underwear drawer Veronique changed. It was her business and her magic.

When Emory's aunt, Lily, announced plans to retire and move to Colorado, Emory jumped at the chance to buy Healing Herbs. People warned against it. Such shops were failing right and left, thanks to the rise of internet shopping, especially those in small towns, but she was determined. She'd loved the place since her aunt opened it twenty years ago, and her best friend, Lene, lived in Deepwood and owned the bookstore next door. What better job for a natural born witch with a talent for crafting spells than running an herb shop?

So she'd sold her condo in Seattle and bought a crumbling Victorian near the shop, sight unseen. She'd packed her belongings, rented a U-Haul, loaded Fred in the car, and moved south.

The naysayers were proved right. The shop had struggled, limping along for a year despite every effort, every spell, and her endless smudging. But she had refused to give up. And then came Veri Laveau and Dangerous Curves.

Emory would be the first to admit she'd been worried people wouldn't come into an herbal shop that was next to a lingerie shop, and at first it seemed her fears were well founded. Veronique's customers weren't interested in the herb shop, and many of Emory's customers started giving her shop a wide berth, as if fat was contagious.

Then Veri suggested the most brilliant thing: a love magic window display. Emory might be a natural witch, but she knew nothing about love magic. That didn't seem to matter. She was immediately inundated with women from Veronique's shop, begging for romantic advice, looking for herbal tinctures to attract soul mates, and buying out the entire section of books on herbal remedies to improve your sex life. For the first time in years, Healing Herbs was in the black, and Emory saw a future for the little shop.

If that weren't enough, it had been Veronique who'd convinced Lene and Emory to start a circle with her. A coven of natural born witches. Despite Emory's love for Healing Herbs, and all things mystical and magical, she'd never thought to seek out other witches besides her best friend. She hadn't even known Veronique *was* a witch until she invited Emory and Lene to form a coven with her. The three of them got together regularly for rituals and fun. While a coven was best with at least four, the three of them muddled along fine. Emory's life had never been so rich or full. The only thing she didn't have was a man, and frankly she was okay with that.

Mr. Hottie suddenly reappeared. Emory got a good view of that amazing backside before he jumped in his jeep and took off. Maybe she wouldn't mind having a man in her life, after all. Not if he looked like that.

Fred poked his head out of his box in the birdcage and glared at her.

"Yes, I know. I already have a man in my life. I promise not to replace you."

He wiggled his nose in satisfaction and disappeared back inside.

She sighed. Gorgeous men, like the one who'd gone into Veri's shop, did *not* date plus-sized women like her. Still, it was fun to think about.

Lene popped her in the door. "Is he gone?"

"Yup." Unfortunately. He'd been some serious eye candy.

"Good. I'm going to talk to Veronique." She was out the door before Emory could blink.

She returned to the inventory sheet. She was low on rue and oil of angelica, and the soulmate herbal blend she'd whipped up last week was gone, along with all the copies of *Improving Your Sex Life Through Herbal Remedies*. She'd already reordered the book, and new copies would be in tomorrow. Who knew that thing would be so popular? It wasn't like it had a terribly titillating title.

She pulled up the order form on her laptop and added angelica and rue, and doubled the order for red candles. After a moment's thought, she tripled the order for tea tins. At the rate her soulmate blend was flying off the shelves, she'd have to start making batches twice a week.

The bell above the door jangled, and a girl drowning in the world's largest black hoodie came in. A single lock of nearly black hair escaped. To say she looked equal parts sad and militant would be the understatement of the century.

Fred popped out of his box again, chittering excitedly, nose wiggling, eyes fixed on the newcomer. For a nocturnal creature, he sure was feisty today.

"Welcome to Healing Herbs." Emory kept her voice light and non-invasive. The poor thing looked like she might bolt any minute. "Can I help you find something?"

The girl, who couldn't have been much older than eighteen, fidgeted, not moving from the doorway as she shifted from foot to foot and stared at Fred. Arms crossed, she tilted her head, and long, lank locks of hair fell forward to cover her face. Shyness, maybe?

The girl's aura was muddy blues, greens, and reds, which indicated insecurity, fear of the future, blame, and anger. Nothing Emory couldn't see just by looking at her physical being. The dark, muddy gray overlaying it all concerned her though. It meant the young woman was holding onto things, and that could result in long-term health problems. This woman needed help. Problem was, would she accept help? Was it even Emory's place to give it?

Even more interesting was the faint shimmer to her aura that spoke of one thing: witchblood.

Auras came in every color of the rainbow. Each color and combination spoke to different parts of a person's personality or psyche. The only auras that shimmered were those of natural born witches, like herself, Lene, and Veri.

"Never mind," the girl said finally, thrusting her chin out. There was the fighter Emory had suspected lurked beneath. "I think I'm in the wrong place."

She wasn't. Emory sensed she'd meant to come into the shop, but now she was freaked out and ready to run. So

25

she did the one thing that came to mind. "No worries. It happens all the time." It didn't. The people who came to Healing Herbs needed to be there for one reason or another. "Before you go, would you like to sit and have a cup of tea?"

"Nah, I don't like tea." But she didn't leave. She fidgeted, shifting back and forth, gaze darting nervously from Emory to the door.

"I've got cookies."

That did it. "Um, okay. Whatever."

Emory busied herself with the electric kettle and delicate china she kept behind the front desk. If you were going to drink tea, you should do it from a proper cup. Mugs were for coffee.

Fred had returned to his box satisfied Emory was taking proper care of their guest.

Emory kept up a light chatter as she poured her special blend into two cups. This one wasn't for finding soulmates. It was for the soothing of one's soul and finding truth. "Such nice weather we've been having, don't you think?"

"I guess." The girl huddled deeper into the hoodie. Emory was starting to think she had the air conditioning on too high, what with people running around in heavy coats and whatnot.

As she poured hot water over the tea leaves, she whispered a subtle incantation for relaxation and a feeling of safety. Couldn't hurt. "I love this time of year. It warms up, things are blooming. It's a good time for new beginnings, don't you think?" She glanced over her shoulder.

The girl gave her a look that clearly said she thought Emory was crazy. "Um, sure." Her tone was more "whatever, lady."

"This way." She carried the teacups over to the small alcove. The comfy, overstuffed chairs were about as relaxing as it got. She set the cups down on the coffee table and sank into a chair, waving her visitor to the other. "Take a load off."

The girl plopped inelegantly into the chair opposite Emory, knees splayed, booted feet practically kicking the coffee table. But her fingers twisted nervously in her lap, giving her away. She leaned forward suddenly, crabbed a cookie off the delicate pink and yellow china plate, and crammed it in her mouth.

Despite the dark hair hanging over half her face, and the too-big hoodie hiding her figure, not to mention the crumbs scattered down her front, Emory could tell she was a naturally pretty girl with the potential to be downright beautiful. Curvy like Emory, Veri, and Lene. Emory wondered if she shopped at Dangerous Curves. Somehow she doubted it. She couldn't see this girl having an interest in wearing a red lace bra set. But one never knew. People could be surprising.

She picked up her tea, the delicate scent of elder flower, rose hips, and chamomile teasing her nose. The first sip was always the best. She sighed, enjoying the feel of the warm liquid sliding down her throat. Her visitor sipped her own tea, and almost immediately there was a visible change. She relaxed and stopped fidgeting.

"Isn't that better?"

The girl shrugged and took another sip. "It's okay." She seemed to remember something. "Thank you." But it wasn't exactly heartfelt.

"Thank you for taking the time to share it with me." Emory gave her a broad smile, which the girl returned. "My name is Emory Chastain. What's yours?" Again, she kept her tone light, unobtrusive. No pressure here.

The girl thought it over. "Mia."

"It's nice to meet you, Mia. Why don't you tell me why you came in today?"

Mia cleared her throat. "It's about a dead body."

CHAPTER
THREE

Noah Laveau ignored the buxom blonde leering at him through the window of the herbal shop next to Veri's. As long as he'd been around, and that was more years than he cared to remember, he'd gotten lots of women's stares. Men's, too, if he were honest. And buxom blondes weren't really his type.

Something stirred behind the blonde, and he caught a flash of pale skin and wild, strawberry curls. He very nearly stumbled to a halt. Only years of practice kept him moving in the right direction. Curvaceous redheads with skin like moonlight, on the other hand, were very much his type..

Pushing open the door to Dangerous Curves, Noah was met with a rush of cool air perfumed with cinnamon and roses, his cousin Veronique's signature scent. She claimed it aroused carnal senses and encouraged her customers to buy more of her frothy fripperies.

Racks upon racks of brightly colored silks, satins, and chiffons crowded the small but elegant space. Raspberry-and-cream striped curtains marked the fitting area, and matching chairs stood at elegant angles nearby for bored husbands or long-suffering best friends. How any straight man could be bored in a place like this was beyond Noah's imagining. It was the sort of place where fantasies came true.

A middle-aged woman with dark hair just going gray gawped at him, her arms filled with bras in every color, which she clutched to her chest like a lifeline.

He nodded to her. "Ma'am."

Looking like she might pass out, she squeaked and darted behind a curtain. He sighed. He was used to that reaction, too. Somebody had once told him he should be a model. Noah would rather French-kiss a Zagan demon, acid spit and all.

"Noah!"

Speak of the devil. Veronique rushed across the shop. Well, more like sashayed. Veronique Laveau did not rush anywhere for anything. She strode with purpose and attitude. She gave him a warm hug. Her brown eyes, flecked with molten gold, danced with joy.

"Are you on leave? When did you get here?" The words rushed out, tumbling over each other. Noah smiled for the first time in a very long while. Of all his many cousins, she was by far his favorite.

He chucked her under the chin. "I'm out, kid." She may be a grown woman, but she was still his baby cousin.

"Out of the Army?" Her eyes widened. "For good? No more trips to Iraq or wherever?"

He tried to smile, but his mouth wouldn't cooperate. "Afghanistan. Nope. I'm done. Thought I'd swing by for a visit. Catch up."

She eyed him shrewdly. It was hard to pull the wool over Veri's eyes. "But you love the Army."

He shrugged, oozing casual. "Sure, but it was time. I've done my part. More than my part." He'd served in not just one, but two desert wars. "Time to move on to the next thing."

Her eyes narrowed to slits. She wasn't buying it. He'd been afraid of that.

"What's going on, Noah?"

"Can't I visit my cousin without getting grilled?" He kept his tone much lighter than he felt.

"Sure." She crossed her arms over her ample chest and tapped one stiletto-shod foot. It made no sound on the plush gray carpet, but Noah could have sworn he felt it in his gut. "If that's really why you're here."

"Why else would I be here?"

She snorted and strode back to the register. "Oh, I can't imagine."

He followed her, oddly feeling like a chastised little boy. Her mother had always had the same effect on him. All the Laveau women did. Fierce was an understatement. "Everything's fine, Veri. I'm just here for a visit. That's all."

"How long?"

"A week, maybe two."

She sighed. "Fine. You don't want to tell me the truth, I get it. I'm hurt, but I get it." She wasn't pouting exactly, but it was close. Her full lower lip gave an exaggerated quiver. "Wait here." She rustled in the cupboard behind her, then placed a key in his palm. "That's my spare house key."

"Alarm code?"

She smirked. "No alarm."

"Veri—" How many times had he told her to get an alarm?

31

"Don't get your panties in a bunch, Noah. I put up wards. Heckuva lot better than any old alarm system. And don't worry. I made sure you're excluded from the 'thou shalt not pass' list."

"Gee, thanks," he said wryly.

"Anytime. Make yourself at home. Beer in the fridge."

He grinned. "You're too good to me."

"I know. And Noah?"

"What?"

"Don't do anything stupid."

He gave her an innocent look. "Don't know what you're talking about."

She snorted and turned her back on him, but Noah wasn't fooled any more than he'd fooled her. That was the problem with family. They always had your back. Even when you didn't want them to.

"Excuse me?" Emory blinked at Mia over the rim of her cup. Even the delicate aromas of honey and jasmine weren't enough to kill the shock. "Did you say 'dead body'?"

Mia rubbed her forehead as if she were in pain. For the first time, she looked more like the vulnerable teen Emory believed she was than the kid with a chip on her shoulder. "Do you believe in..." She hesitated. "Do you believe in visions?" It came out in a rush.

"I believe there are more things in this world than we can explain," Emory said carefully. *Just how much does this girl know? And can she be trusted?* If she'd grown up in Deepwood, she probably knew a lot, but she'd never seen Mia before.

"That didn't answer my question," Mia said, shooting her a belligerent glare.

"Okay then." Emory took a sip of her tea. It had an immediate calming effect.. She glanced over at Fred, whose fuzzy butt was pointed straight at her. "I do. Why?"

"I've been having them lately. All the time."

"What do you see?"

She glanced around. "This shop." She eyed Emory. "You."

"And a dead body?"

"Yes."

Oh goodie. Just what she needed. Dead bodies popping up willy-nilly. "Do you know who it is? Or where the body is?"

Mia shrugged with an air of bravado. "I don't know who. I never see the face. But it's here in this shop. With you."

"Excuse me?" She knew she sounded like a broken record, but she felt foggy, as if her mind had been wrapped in cotton. She wasn't a truthwalker, so she had no idea if Mia was crazy, lying, or had seen a vision. She wasn't a mistwalker either, so she couldn't offer to walk Mia's thoughts and see them for herself. Unless Mia had a spell placed on her, Emory didn't see how she could be of any help.

"It's just what I see," Mia snarled around another mouthful of cookie.

"Okay," Emory said slowly, trying to decide how to handle the situation. She'd had a lot of weird situations thrown at her, but this took the cake. "Well, as you can see, there aren't any dead bodies here."

They glanced around the empty shop. Nothing to see but herbs and spices, candles and tinctures, and the odd stack of books. She glanced out the window and across the street to Pink Lady Donuts, suddenly craving cake—although donuts would do. She bet Virgil didn't have to deal with this sort of thing. A cranky customer when he ran out of maple bars, maybe, but certainly not dead bodies and spooky visions.

Mia shrugged again. "Whatever."

"Have you, ah, told your parents about these visions?"

"Don't have any." Mia had become even more sullen, if that were possible.

Interesting. Emory glanced out the window again. Had Mia's parents been witches who died before passing on their knowledge to their daughter? This definitely required further investigation.

"Are you... did you grown up here? In Deepwood?"

"Nah. Moved here after I turned eighteen. Dunno why." She frowned and grabbed another cookie. "It just... it looked nice."

So she'd been drawn here, probably by her magic. She may not know about witches. Emory fidgeted, wondering how much to say.

A man stumbled into view in front of Healing Herbs. She and Mia started, and Fred dashed wildly back and forth in his cage. Mia actually sloshed tea on her jeans, hissing as the hot liquid soaked through to her skin. The man staggered to the shop door, and they winced as the bell jangled harshly.

The man paused inside the doorway, clutching his throat. He zeroed in on Emory and took a couple of awkward steps, his hand stretched out toward her. The door banged shut behind him, and Emory jumped about a foot.

"Cure," he grated, sounding half strangled.

Snapping out of her shock, she set her cup down, got up, and hurried toward him. "Sir, what's wrong?"

He swayed toward her and grabbed her upper arms so hard, she knew he'd leave a mark. He gave her a shake that sent them both crashing into one of the displays. Bars of soap and tins of tea scattered across the floor. Glass shattered, shards flying. One hit her cheek, slicing deep. Warm blood spilled down her face.

Mia let out a cry and clutched her hand. Bright red seeped through the girl's fingers.

"Go sit down," Emory ordered her. "Apply pressure to the cut and keep it elevated above your heart. I'll be with you as quick as I can." She turned back to the man.

His knees gave out, and he crashed to the floor. She flinched as he hit the floorboards hard. "Cure." His fingers tightened until her arm turned numb.

"A cure for what? Have you been poisoned? Mia," she shouted to the girl, who'd managed to stumble back to the alcove. Blood still seeped from the cut on her hand. "Never mind." She fished around in her pocket, finally locating her phone, intent on dialing 911.

The man squeezed her arm. "No. Magic."

Leaning forward, she smelled something on him. Like a cologne, but more insidious and unpleasant. She sniffed. He reeked of spellwork. Something bad.

She slid the phone back in her pocket. "What kind of magic? Who did this?"

The man stared up at her. "Too late."

"I'm sorry."

His eyes were already glazing over.

Mia appeared beside her. "This is it," she whispered, face white.

Emory frowned. "What?"

"I told you. This is what I saw in my vision."

Emory guessed that answered her question. Mia wasn't lying, and she wasn't crazy. She now had a dead body on her hands, and the stink of magic was all over it.

The shop was a wreck, and both she and Mia bore the marks of an attack. With her luck, the police would immediately suspect one or both of them had something to do with the man's death, so she did the only thing she could. She called Edwina.

Edwina Gale was the owner of Norma's Diner, located a few blocks away. She was also a witch, although not natural born like Emory. She'd come to it later in life, after serving in the military and finding her way to Deepwood, as many of their kind eventually did.

"Emory, my dear, so lovely to hear from you," she said. "Did you hear about the Edwardian Grande Feast next month? I think it will be a marvelous experience. You really should come. I have the perfect gown picked out." Edwina was a fan of historical costuming and events. It was how they'd met.

"I'll try, but Edwina, that's not why I called." Her hand was shaking. Mia stared at her from the alcove, her expression a hollow mask. Not a great way to be introduced to the world of magic.

"Something has happened." Edwina's tone was matter-of-fact. She was not a person given to dramatics or hysterics.

Emory cleared her throat. "You could say that." She gave Edwina a rundown on the death of the man, leaving out the part about Mia and her vision. She wasn't ready to share that with anyone but her coven. "He reeks of magic, Edy. I'm pretty sure there's some kind of spell involved."

"Which is why he came to you, no doubt."

"Definitely. He kept asking for a cure, but it was too late."

Edwina sighed. "Pity."

"What do I do? Should I call the cops?"

Technically, the Deepwood Police knew about things magical. They were used to dealing with things like invisibility spells combined with peeping-toms or one witch stealing moonflowers from another witch's garden. Petty crimes were dealt with easily enough by the mundane officers. But murder by magical means? She wasn't sure they would know what to do with that.

"If I tell them a spell killed him, they either won't believe me, or they'll think I had something to do with it." They'd probably lock her up and throw away the key, a situation her kind was far too familiar with.

"We don't yet know if it was the spell that killed him," Edwina reminded her. "But you're right. Getting the police involved could get sticky. Nathan is a good man," she said, referring to the police chief, "but he doesn't know diddly about magic. I will be there shortly."

Emory wasn't sure what Edwina could do about it, but everyone knew the woman had skills beyond those of mere mortals. "What should I do in the meantime?"

"Forget what they say on TV about not touching anything. Get that body out of sight."

"Got it. Thanks, Edy."

"Don't mention it. No, really. Don't." She hung up.

Emory hurried over to the door, locking it tight before flipping the closed sign. Lene had the spare key, so she'd be able to get in, but possible witnesses would be kept at bay. She glanced at Mia, whose wound still needed tending. Now what? She couldn't move the man on her own, and Mia was out of commission.

A light bulb went off. "Stay here," she ordered.

"Not like I could leave. You locked the damn door."

Emory narrowed her gaze. "Language."

"Seriously? There's a dead guy on the floor, your shop's a hot mess, I'm bleeding to death, and you're worried about my language?"

Emory rolled her eyes. "You are not bleeding to death. I'll be right back."

She half jogged through the storeroom in back to the small room where she did some of her best spellwork. It was the size of a typical small bedroom, about eight feet by ten. The walls had been painted purple, the floor and ceiling black. A small alcove on the back wall housed her altar. A metal curio cabinet next to it was jammed with her spellwork accoutrements.

On the floor were several thick, Persian rugs. Her grandfather had collected them over many years. No doubt they were worth something now, but Emory kept them out of love and memory, and because they were cool.

Quickly rolling one up, she hoisted it to her shoulder. Staggering under its weight, she hauled it out front and dumped it on the floor next to the body. She unrolled it and then squatted next to the dead man. A bit of huffing, puffing, shoving, and rolling, and she had him on the carpet. Taking a deep breath, she grabbed the corners of the rug and dragged it, and the body, across the smooth floor to the back room. Thank the Goddess for wood floors.

Mia followed, still clutching her injured hand tightly to her chest. "Aren't we supposed to call the cops? Not touch anything?"

"Do you want me to call the cops?" Emory demanded, wiping sweat off her brow.

"No," Mia squeaked, eyes wide.

"All right then. Let's see to your hand." She fetched the old sewing basket. It sure was getting a lot of use today.

She quickly and efficiently cleaned and bandaged Mia's wound. Fortunately, it was shallow and didn't need stitches. Emory added an herbal salve she'd made herself. She'd imbued it with a quick healing spell. Mia would be fine in no time.

"You better clean up, too," Mia pointed out wryly. "Unless you want a bunch of stupid questions."

Emory touched her cheek. "Good point." She went to the small bathroom. A glance in the mirror told her the police would have definitely been suspicious. Blood had dried on her face, bruises were blooming on her arm from that morning, and her hair was a hot mess. She washed up, applied a bit of salve, and smoothed her hair. Good enough. Returning to the storeroom, Emory knelt beside the dead man and started going through his pockets.

"What are you doing?" Mia asked, horrified. She'd probably seen one too many episodes of *CSI*.

"Trying to find out who he is. That may help us figure out what happened to him."

"Oh." Her voice was faint.

"Why don't you go and have more tea?" Emory suggested gently.

Mia gave the corpse a last, frightened look and disappeared out front. Emory hoped she wouldn't take off, but there wasn't time to worry about that now. She was pretty sure Mia wouldn't call the police, and that was the important thing.

Emory found a wallet in his left pocket. Inside were credit cards, some cash, and his driver's license. His name was Gary Poe, and he was forty-seven years old. His address was in Moreland, one town over. There was a business card with his name on it. Apparently, he'd been an accountant at a firm a few blocks away from Healing Herbs. Probably he'd started having problems at work, realized they were magical in origin, and come over for help.

She'd never seen him before. How had he known what she was or that she could help? Was he a supernatural? It was possible, though she saw no signs. That didn't mean anything, of course. There were many people in the world with witchblood, whether they knew it or not. There were also quite a few with fairy blood, as well. He could even be a

39

shifter of some kind, though Emory doubted it. A shifter likely wouldn't succumb to a spell quite so dramatically. Then again she had no idea what kind of spell had been put on Mr. Poe.

Emory poked her head out to check on Mia. She was curled up in a chair, a death grip on one of the teacups. The cookie plate was empty. Wonder of wonders, Fred was curled up on her lap, and she was stroking his fur like he was a cat.

It was useless to wonder how Fred got out of his cage. He pretty much did what he wanted. What was surprising was that he was letting a stranger hold him. He didn't take to other people much.

She stepped into the store, closing the door behind her. "Hey, Mia." The girl started violently, and Emory held up a hand to placate her as she sank into the other chair. "Why don't you tell me about your vision again? All the details. Don't leave anything out. How did it start?"

Mia set down her cup, all traces of belligerence gone. "I had the first one last week."

"There's been more than one?" That was a terrifying thought.

"Yes." Her expression was tight, the skin around her mouth and nose pinched. It looked like the dark circles under her eyes had been there a while. "There have been three, each one exactly the same. I see this shop and you and that man." She waved at the storeroom. "I see him speak to you, then he falls over dead. That's it." She returned to petting Fred, who'd cuddled into her armpit.

"Nothing else? You don't hear anything?"

"No. Just see it." She closed her eyes as if that might drive away the sight of the body on the shop floor. She opened them, giving Emory a shrewd look. "You're a witch, aren't you?"

She decided the truth would serve her best. "I am. How did you know?"

Mia rolled her eyes in the way of teenagers worldwide. "It's obvious. This town is positively stuffed with them."

So she knew the town's secret. "Are you a witch?"

Mia shrugged. "Maybe. My mom was a little weird."

Was. So the girl's mother was dead or gone. But what about her father? Before Emory could say anything else, the lock rattled, the door crashed open, and Lene stormed in. Her face was flushed. Fred startled, bounced out of Mia's lap, and scurried back to his cage.

"Okay," Lene said to the room at large. "Where's the dead body?"

Potions, Poisons and Peril

CHAPTER
FOUR

Emory was certain Mia was on the verge of bolting. She patted the girl's arm in a desperate attempt at reassurance. "That's just my friend, Lene. She owns the bookstore next door. She's kind of a lot, but you get used to it."

Lene's eyes narrowed, and her hot pink painted lips turned down. "What's that supposed to mean?"

"Listen, we've got a situation on our hands," Emory said, heading her off.

"I can sense that." Lene relocked the door. "Dead body?"

Lene wasn't just any witch. She was a deathwalker, a type of witch nearly as rare as a spellwalker. She sensed when death was near, which meant she could find bodies people didn't want found. Sometimes she knew when someone would die, never a fun thing. There were those who claimed a particularly powerful deathwalker could actually raise the dead ala necromancy, although that was just an old wives' tale as far as anyone knew. Lene had certainly never done it.

Emory pulled Lene aside and gave her a quick rundown of Gary Poe's sudden demise. "Edwina is coming."

"Good. Maybe she can do something. Last thing we need are the cops poking around. Especially with you looking like that."

"Gee, thanks." Emory touched the bandage on her cheek.

"You're welcome. What about her?" Lene jerked her head in Mia's direction.

"She had a vision."

"Seriously?"

"Yup. She saw the guy die in my shop. Not just once but three times. In visions, I mean. He only died once."

Lene squinted, giving Mia the once-over. "Witchblood?"

Emory shrugged. "Maybe. Probably." Now was not the time to try and figure that out. "Whatever she is, she's freaked out. We need her calm and cooperative. Maybe she saw something in her visions than can help us find out who killed Gary Poe."

"And we don't want to lose track of a possibly powerful witch," Lene said with an arch look.

She had that right. Although witchblood wasn't rare, a true natural born witch was, especially powerful ones like Lene, Emory, and Veri. If Mia was a witch, she was probably a strong one, and they needed to find out where her alliances lay. Powerful witches running amok were never a good idea, even in a town like Deepwood.

"I'll clean up while we wait," Lene said. "You find out as much as you can about the girl."

Emory returned to the alcove while Lene righted the fallen table and piled soap on it. Someone pounded on the door. All three of them looked up. Emory peered through the glass and saw umber eyes staring at her. In front of him stood Veri.

"Holy Hades, it's the hottie," Emory gasped. "Where'd he come from?"

"He's Veri's cousin," Lene said smugly. "He was in the army and just got back from Afghanistan. He's staying with her for a while. When I sensed the dead body, she called him."

Emory had no idea why Veri would do that. Just because he was a soldier didn't mean he knew a darn thing about hiding dead bodies. How the heck were they going to explain this? "Fabulous." She unlocked the door. "We're going to have half of Deepwood in here."

Veri sashayed in first with a swish of her vintage tangerine skirts, coolly scanning the store. Her white strappy heels clicked loudly on the hardwood floor as she skirted bits of glass. "Where is it?"

"Where's what?" Emory played dumb.

"The body, of course. Lene said there was one here. I brought Noah to help."

So that's his name. Emory tried to pretend indifference. *And Goddess, is it a sexy one.* Dark eyes fastened on her, and she felt his gaze all the way to her bones.

She cleared her throat. "Noah, hello. Welcome to Healing Herbs. I'm Emory Chastain, the owner." It sounded weird, in the midst of a crisis, to introduce herself like she was at a tea party, but she had no idea what else to do. Why did Veri think he could help? Emory held out her hand, and he took it. The moment their fingers touched, it was like fireworks going off behind her eyelids.

She jerked her hand away, suddenly breathless. "It's, ah, nice to meet you," she finally managed.

"You, as well," he said, watching her carefully.

His voice was a low, gravelly rumble that intensified whatever crazy thing was going on with her. It felt like sparks were skipping off her fingertips, so she tucked her hands behind her back. "I'm not sure how you can help—"

"Don't worry. This isn't my first dead body."

Noah had just kicked up his feet in front of Veri's TV, a frosty beer in one hand and the remote in the other, when his cell phone buzzed. With a groan of annoyance, he snagged it off the end table. "What?"

"I need your help." It was Veri. She sounded a little freaked out.

"What happened?"

"My friend, Lene, is here," Veri said. "Lene is a deathwalker."

His blood ran cold. A witch who could sense death. Sometimes impending, sometimes *fait accompli*. He'd had no idea Veri knew anyone that powerful, although he shouldn't have been surprised. Like to like. "And?"

"There's a dead body next door," she blurted. "Emory's over there alone. I'm afraid."

"Where are you?" He was already up and getting his boots back on. He gave the beer a longing glance. It would have to wait.

"My shop, but I'm headed to Emory's. It's the herbal place."

"On my way."

"Hurry."

The drive to the herb shop was a tense one. His knuckles were white on the steering wheel. Scenarios ran through his head, none of them good. If someone hurt Veri, well, he would hunt down whoever it was and make sure he or she never hurt another soul.

He pulled up at Veri's shop with a screech of tires and jumped out almost before the engine shut off. She was standing outside the herb shop waiting for him. Impatience strummed through even line of her body. They entered the shop together.

He spotted the buxom blonde from earlier, and next to her was the luscious redhead he'd seen in the shop window. She was stunning, one of the most beautiful women he'd seen in a long time. She gazed at him with big, blue eyes, and he could have sworn his heart stopped beating before it kicked in again so hard, he heard it throbbing in his ears.

Through the buzzing in his head, he heard Veri introduce him. The redhead said something and held out her hand, which he took. The buzzing intensified, and he was suddenly short of breath. The redhead said something else, but he couldn't seem to focus on her words.

He blurted out the first thing that came into his head. "Don't worry. This isn't my first dead body."

Potions, Poisons and Peril

CHAPTER FIVE

Emory stared at the man still holding her hand. She wouldn't say the world faded away or anything equally corny, but she definitely had little interest in anything but Noah in that precise moment. He appeared to be similarly affected. *What the heck is going on?* Finally he released her hand, and it was like she could breathe again.

"N-not your first?" she stammered, feeling like an idiot. *How many dead bodies has he seen?* He'd been at war, so probably a lot.

"Not at all." He gave her a smile that made her feel flushed all over. "How can I help?"

She licked her lips, throat suddenly dry. "No need. Edwina's coming." Immediately she felt like slapping herself. Why had she said that? Why? Why couldn't she just flutter her eyelashes and accept his help like a normal person? Goddess, why was she suddenly so hopeless at this flirting business? Although flirting while stashing a corpse in your storeroom was probably a bad idea anyway.

"Edwina's coming?" Veri frowned.

"Do you mean Edwina Gale?" Noah asked. "The woman who runs the diner?"

"Yes and yes. Why?" Emory asked. Veri shrugged as if it were no big deal, so Emory turned to Noah. "Do you know her?"

"She makes good pie. But what's she got to do with this dead guy? Why not call the cops?"

"Edwina has a special set of skills, up to and including black belts in half a dozen different martial arts. Believe me, in this instance, she's better than the police," Veri said.

"Until Ms. Gale gets here, why don't you let me take a look at the body," Noah prompted.

"Fine." Emory didn't see what it could hurt. There'd already been a parade of people in her shop who knew about it. She led him to the back room and opened the door. Nobody followed them, not even Veri.

Noah stared n at the prone corpse of Gary Poe. Poor man. Emory felt sorry for him. Poe, not Noah. Her feelings about Noah were something else entirely, but she was trying to ignore those at the moment.

"How did it happen?"

She hugged herself. Was the storeroom cooler than usual? "I was having tea with Mia when he stumbled into the store." She gave him a quick rundown, leaving out the part where Mia was having visions of Poe's death.

He frowned, eyeballing the corpse. "Poison?"

She shook her head. *How much did he know about the supernatural? What was safe to tell him?* "You—ah—how much do you know about Veri?"

"If you're asking about the witch thing, don't worry. I know just about everything there is to know." He gave her a long look. "Including the fact that she's in your coven and Deepwood is basically witch central. So go ahead. Tell me the truth. Is it poison or something else?"

"Acts like poison, but I'm pretty sure it was a spell of some kind. I haven't walked it yet, so I can't be sure."

"Walked it? You're a spellwalker?"

He knows about spellwalkers?

Emory swallowed. Goddess, she had a big mouth. Why had she just blurted that out? Spellwalkers were rare and not exactly welcome in most supernatural circles. In fact, at one point they'd been hunted nearly to extinction, and that was *before* the witch hunts history had made them infamous.

Noah slid a glance in her direction. His face was completely blank, but there was something in his eyes that made her heart flutter. "I will not betray you, Emory. Any more than I would betray my own blood."

Veri, of course. "Fine. Yes, I'm a spellwalker." She smiled grimly and muttered the words social media had recently made famous, the words originally written by her grandmother. "I am the daughter of the ones you didn't burn."

He gave her a long look. "A scan will definitely be useful if he was ensorcelled, as you believe."

Ensorcelled. Now there was a term she hadn't heard in a while. She heard murmuring from the front room, followed by the thud of heavy boots. "Edy's here."

Noah didn't move, didn't so much as bat a smoky eyelash, when Edwina Gale appeared in the doorway. She was an Amazon of a woman, at least six feet tall with the shoulders of a linebacker and built of solid muscle. Her hair, once a rich dark brown, was now streaked with iron gray and tied back in a thick braid. Her gray eyes were bright and intelligent. At sixty-something, she had more strength and energy than Emory had at thirty.

"Heard you have a problem needs seeing to," Edwina said, propping her fists on wide hips. She wore a mint green cotton diner uniform straight out of the '60s, and her feet were shod in shiny purple Doc Martens.

Emory pointed at the body. "You could say that."

Edwina turned to Noah, giving him a once-over. "And you are?"

"Noah Laveau. I'm Veronique's cousin."

Edy snorted and ignored his outstretched hand to squat next to Gary Poe. "Sure, you are." She braced an arm on one knee. "I can disappear him, no worries." She stood.

"Shouldn't we investigate or something?" Emory asked. "If this is a murder, it needs to be solved."

"We don't know it's a murder," Edwina pointed out. "Right now this is just a dead guy."

"Who didn't die by natural means," Emory said. "We can't turn this over to the police, so we need to find out who did this ourselves and stop them from doing it again. Maybe this man has a family. A wife and kids. We can't just hide him and do nothing."

Edwina crossed her arms, her eyes sharp, intense. "Okay, so we investigate, and then what? Take the law into our own hands? Mete out punishment?"

"I don't know," she admitted. "But we have to do something." Maybe they could bring the police into it then. Or maybe they could involve the Witch Council. The Council was the governing body of all magical things that went on in Deepwood. If this turned out to be a spell, they'd be interested.

"*If* it was murder," Edwina pointed out. "And do we know for sure it is?"

"Spellwork killed this man." Emory was confident about that. "I doubt a human could manage that level of magic. Could you?"

Edwina thought about it. "Doubt it. I can weave some basic wards, maybe influence someone's behavior. I once got a coffee for free—"

"Edwina! That's not how magic is meant to be used."

She shrugged, completely unrepentant. "It is what it is."

"Well, see, you're one of the most powerful non-witchblood witches I know, so a human definitely didn't do this."

"But you don't know that for sure," Edwina pointed out.

"I will when I walk it," Emory assured her.

"Then do it now."

She waved a hand. "Not like this. There are too many people. Too much distraction."

Edwina sighed. "Then I'll clear them out so you can work your mojo." She started toward the door, then turned to give Noah a look. It was the kind of look that made lesser men wilt.

Noah didn't even glance Edy's way. His eyes were on Emory. "I'm staying."

Emory shot him a look, startled. A giddy feeling streaked through her, making her feel flushed. *Well, alrighty then.*

With Noah standing guard at the door, Emory carefully walked a circle around Gary Poe's body. She didn't bother with salt or herbs. There was nothing left inside poor Gary to get out. Ninety percent of the time, spells were attached to the victim, no one else. If it was the other 10 percent, nothing in the world was going to keep it from spilling over. The circle was more to keep outside influences from messing up her spellwork.

She sat cross-legged next to Gary and closed her eyes. She let her inner self sink into that place somewhere between being awake and in a trance. She reached it in under a minute. She'd had practice. A lot of it. Then she opened herself up to her ability, allowing it to flow through her unchecked in gentle swells, like the roll of ocean waves. She opened her eyes.

At some point, Fred had joined her. He sat in front of her, nose wiggling, staring at Gary Poe with interest.

Above the body floated dozens of symbols. They were fading fast. She needed to inspect them before they disappeared for good. Whoever had created the spell had done a fine job of it. Not many people thought to put a dissipation spell on top of another spell. She was beginning to think Gary's death had been no accident.

She stood, the symbols dancing around her. She held out her hand, palm up, and one floated into place above it. She didn't recognize it. She'd never seen anything like it in anywhere in all her studies. The second was a seven-pointed star, the symbol for magical energy. That made sense, as the spell would need a lot of energy to accomplish what it had been designed to do. The next symbol was oddly squiggly and, again, indecipherable.

The final symbol drifted into place before winking out a second later, but she'd already seen it: a large X with a small circle in the upper V of the letter. It was the symbol of death.

She must have made a sound, because Noah took a step toward her. "What is it?" he asked.

"This was no ordinary spell. This was premeditated murder."

CHAPTER
SIX

"You're certain someone meant to kill this guy?" Edwina asked as she rolled Gary Poe up in the rug. Noah had offered to help, but she'd given him a dirty look.

Using it to move Poe's body was one thing, but wrapping him up in it? It gave Emory the heebie-jeebies. "Hey, that's my grandfather's rug."

Edwina gave her a disgusted look. "You want I should just carry him around where everyone can see him?"

She sighed. "Good point. Roll away. To answer your question, I need to look deeper at the elements of the spell," she admitted. "But it looks that way, yes." She could always get the rug back later. And clean the heck out of it.

"We can't take this out the front door," Noah said as Edy finished wrapping the body like a macabre candy roll. "Not unless we want the cops asking uncomfortable questions. Even inside a rug, it looks like a body dump."

"You have a back entrance?" Edwina asked Emory.

"There is, but you'd have to walk past every business on the block, plus a row of condos, to get to the street." She wasn't about to ask how Edwina knew about getting rid of bodies.

Edwina shook her head. "No good. We need to get it out unseen. What about the portals?"

Noah's eyes narrowed, but he didn't say anything, which made Emory distinctly uncomfortable. For about the twentieth time she wondered how much he knew about... everything.

The portals were ancient, interdimensional wormholes, for lack of a better word. Magical tunnels that led from this world to others. Some led to other places or time periods in this world. Some led to other planets, some to other universes.

Shortly after they first met, Edwina had asked her about the portals. Emory had been shocked. These days not many remembered them, but Edy had found an old grimoire belonging to a portal witch at a garage sale.

Emory did not want to open the portals. It was uncomfortable and made her skin itch, but Edwina was right. There weren't many options. Even at night, Deepwood was busy enough there was no way they could move a dead body without someone noticing. It was the portals or prison.

"Fine." She sighed. "Where do you want to go?"

"We need to get as far away from here as possible," Edwina said. "Somewhere remote, where no one will find the body for a thousand years. By then, no one will care if he was killed by a spell or not."

"I've got a place in the bayou," Noah spoke up. "They'll never find it there."

"All right. Grab the body and bring it into my spell room." Emory led the way to the back of the storeroom.

Noah hefted Gary Poe onto his shoulder and strode past rows of shelving to the back wall. Edwina followed him. Emory swept aside the curtain hiding her spell room so they could enter.

"You don't need to come," she told Noah.

He ducked through the curtain. Apparently he had no intention of letting her do this on her own. Shaking her head, she followed them into the smaller room, allowing the curtain to fall closed behind her.

"Where should I put him?" Noah asked.

Emory cleared her throat. "Against the wall would be good. I need to work in the center."

Noah lay Poe on the bare floor, which was painted black like the ceiling, while Emory crossed the room toward the green metal curio cabinet against the back wall. Inside were crowded rows of tincture bottles, tins of herbs, multi-colored crystals, and other accoutrements of her trade. Not that she technically needed such things to perform magic. "Magic" flowed through her veins, infusing every cell in her body. The stuff just helped her focus all that energy. They were fun, too.

At some point, Fred had bounced in and perched on top of her cabinet, watching with bright eyes. He wiggled his whiskers at her but stayed silent and out of the way.

She selected a stick of plain white chalk. Waving them to the side of the room, she drew an intricate design in the center. She tried really hard not to look at the body as she drew the complicated, intertwining design. She was going to have enough nightmares as it was.

Once the labyrinthine center symbol was finished, she did the outer edges, sketching the sigils for the portal ways. Symbols that were much older than the memory of human civilization, symbols that belonged only to the witches who guarded the portals. Witches like Emory.

She was one of the few left who could open them, control them. It was a heavy responsibility. Used incorrectly, well, bad things happened. Very bad things.

Finished, Emory returned the chalk to the curio cabinet and selected several white candles. In the circle, she placed one candle on each of the outer symbols, save one.

She paused, the final candle clutched in her hand. "I'm going with you," she said finally, determination in her tone. No way was she allowing Edwina to take care of this alone. This was partly her mess.

Edwina frowned. "I don't like it."

"Non-negotiable," Emory insisted.

"You're the boss." Her eyes twinkled at her little joke. Everyone knew Edwina Gale couldn't be bossed around by anyone.

Emory placed the final candle in the center symbol. Walking back to the cabinet, she grabbed a clay jar filled with salt and then bent down to collect a small, leather satchel filled with supplies. "Remember," she reminded Edwina and Noah, "do not cross the salt line until I tell you. Got it?"

Edwina gave a brief nod, her braid swinging.

Emory turned to Noah and raised a brow. He, too, nodded, so she placed the satchel next to where she would stand, then carefully poured a line of salt in a large circle around the symbols.

"Here goes nothing." She moved toward the center candle. Taking a deep breath, she closed her eyes and chanted. The candle sparked, the wick flamed, and she called the four corners. She felt the tug and pull of the ancient portal system as it caught at her power.

She slowly walked the circle of salt, tracing each symbol with her finger. She could have used her athame, but it wasn't necessary. As she passed each candle, its wick burst into flame, and with each pulse of fire, she felt the pull of the portals grow stronger. She sensed Noah's eyes on her, watching her every move. The flush in her cheeks wasn't just from the heat of the candles.

There was a surge of power as the circle closed, and Emory welcomed the rush that lifted the hairs on the back of her neck. Calling the portals always made her nervous, but she had to admit she was drawn to the power. Returning to the center flame, she resumed chanting the ancient litany taught to her by her grandmother. It was time. Pulling out the vial hanging between her breasts, she uncorked it and downed the contents. The taste was bitter as the liquid burned its way down her throat. She let the vial fall back against her chest, continuing to chant.

The room began to swirl and shimmer, taking on a hazy glow. Sparks danced in the air, hissing and sizzling. An electric charge in the air frizzed her hair and snapped along metal surfaces like the charge before a storm. A barrier coalesced along the salt circle, pinks, blues, and greens rolling across it like the Northern Lights until she could no longer see what was on the other side. Golden sparks danced along the colors before drifting away from the barrier toward the center of the circle.

She held out her hand, and the golden sparks streaked to her, forming an orb in the palm of her hand. The light intensified, nearly blinding her as the orb grew and grew. Streaks of light slammed into the orb until tears streamed down her face, and she had to squint against the brightness.

She stopped chanting. The orb turned lazily above her palm, pulsing in time to the beat of her heart.

With a smile, she closed her eyes, breathed in, and let go. The orb exploded, shattering into a million pieces. When she opened her eyes, a shimmering disc of silver swirled in front of her.

Noah started for Emory, but Edwina grabbed his arm and held him back. There was a surprising amount of strength in her arm for a woman her age. "She said to wait until she gave the okay. Trust me. You want to listen to her on this."

Noah shot her a scowl but stayed put. Edwina was right. He had to wait until Emory gave the all clear. Just like he'd had to wait for his men back in Afghanistan. Or Iraq. Or ancient Persia. But they had been trained warriors, like himself. Emory.... She was a powerful witch who could take care of herself. He had to remind himself of that constantly. There was a time when he'd worked closely with warrior women who were his equal or stronger, but those had been different days. He'd forgotten what that was like. It had taken a long time for women to rediscover their power. Even longer to take it back.

There was a chitter, and he glanced down at Fred, who had jumped off the cabinet. He stood next to the salt line, waiting patiently as if he knew. But that was ridiculous. He was a chinchilla, for crying out loud.

Emory finally turned to them. She was a little pale but otherwise untouched. "All right," she said. "It's safe." She leaned down for her satchel, and Fred bounced forward and jumped up on her shoulder, riding it like a pirate's parrot.

As he picked up Poe, Noah said, "That was... interesting." He could have kicked himself for being so lame, but it was the first thing that came into his head. Never had a woman left him so tongue-tied.

"It's what I do. I suggest you avoid touching the walls while we're inside."

He lifted an eyebrow.

"Let's just say they have a habit of giving travelers a nasty shock. Ready?" she said.

Edwina strode past them, stepping through the portal first as if she'd used them many times before. Emory followed her. Noah took a deep breath, adjusted the body slung across his shoulders, and plunged in.

He wasn't sure what he expected. A sucking vortex maybe? But it was no different than stepping from one room into the next. One moment he was standing in Emory's shop, and the next he was inside some sort of tunnel. It reminded him of a wormhole from a sci-fi movie. It was a long, gently curving tube with walls that swirled in blues and greens and what looked like fluffy white clouds. It was just wide enough to walk two abreast and was at least two feet higher than his six foot four.

"Are you coming?" Emory snapped impatiently, Fred chittering from her shoulder.

He hurried after her. "How will you know where to go?"

"The portal will show me."

The tunnel curved to the right before branching into three tubes. Emory followed Edwina into the left branch, Noah hot on their heels. They branched right after that and then left again, stopping before an arched doorway. Beyond it Noah saw the dim, green light and bald cypress trees dripping with Spanish moss that indicated they'd reached the bayou. He heard the faint roar of a 'gator and the call of birds as a warm, humid breeze swirled around him.

"We're here," Emory said needlessly. "Watch your step." She disappeared from view, Fred's bushy tail waving in the air.

"This is your land?" Emory asked Noah as she stepped out of the portal into twilight gloom. The heat and humidity were oppressive, like stepping into a steamy shower. The air was heavy with dank, moldy things.

Fred curled up under her hair. Chinchillas weren't fond of heat or light.

Noah nodded. "Been in my family for hundreds of years."

"Come on, you two," Edwina said. "We have a job to do. Where to, Noah?"

He took the lead, striding along what Emory assumed was a path, Poe bouncing on his shoulder. Not a single sight or sound of civilization penetrated this deep into the wilderness. She slapped at a bug that landed on her bare arm. Noah was right. No one would ever find Poe here.

Her sandals weren't made for the rough terrain of the bayou. The grasses and brush scraped her feet and ankles, leaving bloody scratches, and she was up to her ankles in mud. She refused to so much as wince. No way was she letting Noah or Edwina send her back.

Not that they could. She controlled the portals.

Noah tromped easily over the uneven ground, Poe draped across his shoulders like a sack of potatoes. He didn't look back to see if they were still following. His sole focus was somewhere down the path she could barely make out. Every now and then, she snuck glances at him, trying not to stare too openly at a face the goddess herself must have crafted. It really wasn't fair of Her to make a man so beautiful. Emory heaved a sigh.

"Are you all right?"

She started as Noah's deep voice intruded on her inner ramblings. "Uh, yeah. Just, you know, these sandals weren't made for hiking."

"You should have said something." He stared at her feet with a frown.

"It's no big deal. Besides, what would you have done?"

"I don't know. Carried you."

She snorted. "*And* a dead body?"

"Would the two of you stop messing around?" Edwina said lightly. "At this rate it'll take a week to bury him."

Potions, Poisons and Peril

CHAPTER
SEVEN

After what seemed like an eternity, Noah stopped in a clearing nearly surrounded by water. It was nearly dark. The thick foliage which had turned daylight to twilight now turned the fading sun to dusk.

Noah heaved Poe to the ground. "This is a good spot."

"How the heck did you carry a body this far without getting winded?" Emory demanded. He looked cool as a cucumber. Between the humidity and sweat, she probably looked like a drowned rat.

"You should try carrying an army pack around the desert."

Edwina pulled a couple folding shovels out of her pack. She thrust one at Noah. "Over here next to the tree is as good a spot as any."

Emory rolled her eyes. Nobody would notice if they'd buried it anywhere between the portal and here with a big sign: Body Buried Here. There wasn't anyone around for miles, as far as she could tell. Only alligators, wild birds, and a lot of moss.

"I can help," she said, stepping forward to take a shovel.

Edwina chuckled. "No offense, but you're not exactly strong in the upper body department. And those sandals..." She shook her head.

Emory glared at her. "I can still do my fair share." Fred gave a chitter that sounded suspiciously disparaging.

"We'll get it done a lot faster if Noah and I do it. No offense, Em, but you are not the outdoorsy type."

"Then what am I supposed to do? Stand around like some helpless damsel? I don't think so."

"Unless you can use magic to dig a hole, I don't see you that have much choice," Edwina said.

She didn't, though that would have been a heck of a lot more useful than some of the spells she knew. An idea popped into her mind. "I'll review the spell more carefully. See what I can glean from what I saw."

"How?" Noah asked.

Emory smiled. "With art."

She pulled a small sketch journal and a makeup bag filled with colored drawing pencils out of her satchel. While Noah and Edwina dug, she sat with her back against a tree trunk, opened her journal, took a deep breath, and began to draw.

Fred kept her company, letting out the occasional squeak. Now and then, he'd dart off to inspect something, then bounce back, his cheeks stuffed with a fresh berry or some other tidbit.

First she sketched each symbol as and where she'd seen it. Sometimes the location of the symbol in connection with the person relayed as much as its location in regard to the other symbols.

Once each sigil was sketched, she added color. Color said a lot, too. A reddish cast could mean passion or rage. Black, the absence of color, usually meant evil intent. Pure white was rare. She'd only see it once in a protection spell a mother had placed on her child. It meant pure love and intent.

The symbols around Gary Poe had been mostly shades of green, ranging from verdant to bilious. She'd never seen it before, and it piqued her curiosity. Once all the symbols were colored, she placed the journal open on the grass and stared at what she'd drawn.

Noah and Edwina had stopped digging, having decided the hole was deep enough.

"Those are Viking symbols," Edwina said, peering at the drawing.

""Some of them are. It looks like they've been mixed with Celtic and Greek and something else, though I'm not sure what."

"Sumerian," Noah said.

She glanced at him, startled. "That's a dead language. Like, way dead. It probably hasn't been spoken by a living person in thousands of years."

"Not entirely true," he said, face impassive.

"You know someone who speaks Sumerian?"

He cleared his throat. "I do."

"Can you contact this person? Get a translation for me?"

He opened his mouth to speak.

"How about we bury this dead guy first?" Edwina interrupted. "Kinda why we came here."

They finished burying Gary Poe. After they'd washed the dirt off their hands in the water Noah had assured them was safe. Although eager to get back to her shop, and hopefully Mia if she was still there, Emory suggested they have a small service.

"It doesn't seem right to just leave him here."

Edwina agreed. "Can't have his spirit wandering around, giving people a fright."

She moved to stand at the head of the grave, Edwina and Noah taking up positions on either side of it. Fred sat on Emory's foot as if presiding over the ceremony. She invoked a small spell to help Gary Poe's spirit cross to the Other Side.

"A time to live,
A time to die.
May the spirits guide you
To the Other Side.
Go in peace
And blessed thee.
As I will
So mote it be."

"So mote it be," Edwina echoed.

After a moment Noah broke the silence. "Ready to go?"

"Yes," Emory said, turning toward the portal, Fred once again perched on her shoulder.

"What should we do next?" Emory asked as they stepped back into her spell room.

Fred scrambled down and bounced off to his cage.

"Don't ask me," Edwina said as Emory closed the portal. "You wanted a body gotten rid of, I helped you do that. This is your investigation."

When did this become my investigation? "What if I need you again?"

"You know I'm always here for you, but it's getting late, and I left the diner in my nephew's dubious care. I gotta get a shower and spruce up. Séance tonight." Edwina disappeared through the curtain.

Emory had always found it odd that Edwina held tarot readings and séances at a diner. It didn't exactly have... atmosphere. But that was Edwina for you. She did what she wanted and didn't much care about things like ambiance or if it was the right way to do a thing.

Noah started to follow her, but Emory grabbed his arm. "That symbol. Can you find out what it means?" She flipped open her journal and pointed to the one he'd told her was Sumerian.

"Possibly. I'll make a quick call."

"Won't your friend need to see it?"

"I guess." He pulled a phone out of his pocket and snapped a picture. "I'll email it."

"Let me know as soon as you have the answer. Please."

He gave her a long look. "Sure."

She stashed her satchel next to the curio cabinet, then went to the front room, Noah on her heels. Fred was already curled up in the birdcage, the door standing wide open. She tried to ignore the heat of Noah's stare burning a hole in her back.

Lene and Veri were seated in the alcove, sipping tea and munching on biscuits. They'd wrangled Edwina into joining them, despite her pressing need to get back to her store. There was no sign of Mia.

Emory selected an almond from her stash and dropped it in Fred's dish. He uncurled and helped himself to the treat, whiskers twitching wildly.

"Where's Mia?" Emory asked.

"I offered to take her home," said Lene, "but she cussed me out and left on her own. Don't worry. I got her info first. She was just really freaked out, and I thought it was better not to overwhelm her any more than we already have."

She had to agree with the decision. It wouldn't have been her first option, but no doubt the girl needed time on her own to regroup. It was a witch thing. They would track Mia down later.

"How did things go?" Veri asked, eying her over the lip of her cup.

"Well as can be expected. The, ah, item is buried where no one will ever find it."

"We hope," Lene said drily.

"It won't be," Noah assured them.

"I wish I could be sure," Emory muttered.

"If you buried it where I think you did, be sure," Veri said, selecting another cookie.

"I'm worried, though. What if friends or family come looking for him? They're going to have questions," Emory pointed out.

"We can do a search for him online," Lene said, pulling her phone out. She frowned a little as she concentrated on swiping through the internet. "He's on several social media sites," she chirped. "Oh, that's sad. He's got like twenty friends. Most of them are work colleagues." Lene had always been tenderhearted.

"No family?" Veri asked.

"None that I can see."

"Hopefully we can find out more when we search his place," Emory said.

70

Veri said, "Who's this 'we?' I'm not breaking into anyone's house."

"Are you sure you want to get involved, Emory? This could be dangerous," Lene said in a low voice.

"I'm sure." She needed to know who'd done this and why. That need burned in her veins, and she knew she couldn't let it go. "Edwina, can you help?"

"I suppose. In for a penny, in for a pound, as they say. I could visit the victim's home and workplace. See what I can dig up. Anything I should know before I go?"

"I'm still waiting on Noah's contact to explain the last symbol so I can translate the spell. I'm guessing it's going to be important. We might want to wait to search his house until we know what we're dealing with. If we step into something we don't understand— Let's just say it could be bad."

"How long?" Edwina barked at him.

He gave her a long look, his expression shuttered. "I'll let you know when I hear anything."

"Well, light some fires if you need to." She snagged the last cookie and strode to the door. "Time's wasting."

Noah's tone was dry as dust. "I'll see what I can do."

The door banged shut behind Edwina, and Noah took the chance to pull out his phone and look at the screen. "Looks like my contact came through." He glanced at Emory, whose eyes lit up. Oh, gods of the deep, she was gorgeous.

"What does it mean?" she asked, edging closer to look at the email.

Noah quickly tucked his phone away. He did not want her to know he'd lied. There was no email. No contact. He'd known the meaning of the ancient symbol the moment he'd laid eyes on it. There were those who remembered the ancient languages. "Compliance, more or less."

He could see things snap into place in her mind. She smiled. "It all makes sense." Her smile faltered. "And yet it makes no sense at all."

"Clarify," he barked before reminding himself she wasn't one of his soldiers. "Please," he added. He liked the way she nibbled on her lower lip while she mulled it over.

She didn't seem to notice his barking or his stare. She was too wrapped up in the mystery. "This spell wasn't meant to kill Poe after all."

"It wasn't?"

She shook her head, strawberry ringlets dancing around her face. His fingers itched to touch those curls. Caress them. He ordered his hormones under control. He was a soldier, not some untried youth.

"Many of the symbols are the same," she said, "but that one changes things. It flips the meanings of some of the other symbols, especially when combined with the shades of green."

"All right, I'll bite," Veri said. "What was the spell supposed to do?"

"It wasn't meant to be deadly. It was meant to make the ensorcelled compliant. Open to the orders of the spellcaster."

Noah frowned. "Why? I mean, I can think of a lot of ways that would come in handy, but why this guy? And to what end?"

"I have no idea," she admitted. "He shouldn't have died from that spell. Maybe we can find something at his home that will help me understand it better."

"I take it that means you're going with Edwina," Noah said.

"You better believe it." She already had her phone out, texting.

"I'll go, too," Noah said.

"I don't know—"

"I'm going."

Emory scowled. "Guess that settles it, then."

Noah grinned. "Guess it does."

Potions, Poisons and Peril

CHAPTER
EIGHT

Gary Poe lived in a vintage cottage in Moreland, the swanky village a few miles away from the quirkier, trendier, and more magical Deepwood. It was known for its leafy green streets and rambling old houses, most of which had a European or East Coast feel. Small cottages were rare in the extreme, but somehow Gary Poe had found one.

It was built on a smallish lot wedged between a massive blue Cape Cod and a rambling faux Tudor in an unfortunate shade of brown. Across the street was an Italianesque villa, complete with red tile roof (ridiculous in Pacific Northwest weather), cream stucco walls, and an ornate fountain out front. Water spewed in an endless cycle from the lips of a winged cherub clutching a bunch of grapes. Emory found the thing a bit overdone.

They'd gone their separate ways after the burial so they could shower and change. Noah had gotten into the spirit of things with a black T-shirt and utility pants. Edwina was wearing a peach version of her waitressing uniform, with her purple boots, and Emory had opted for flowing palazzo pants—black in a nod to their clandestine adventure—and a pink, ruffled peasant blouse.

Edwina used the keys they'd found in Poe's pocket to unlock the front door. Nobody seemed to notice strangers were entering a neighbor's house. Maybe no one was home.

She missed Fred's warm presence, but she wasn't about to take him to the house of a murder victim. What if there was danger? She'd never forgive herself if something happened to the little guy.

Poe's home was neat as a pin. The oak floors were highly polished and free of scratches or dents, as if they'd been recently laid. Except Emory was pretty sure they were original. The lath-and-plaster walls were painted stark white and devoid of pictures or paintings. The furniture looked like it had been acquired from the same collection at IKEA. Everything was stylishly comfortable with a classic-meets-modern feel, and it all matched. The place should have been cute and cozy, but it felt impersonal and soulless. Emory preferred the perfectly imperfect Zen of mismatched couches, bold colors, and vintage finds.

"Split up," she said. "Check every room. We're looking for anything that would give us a clue to what poor Gary was into or why someone would put a spell on him."

Noah and Edwina nodded. The latter disappeared up the stairs to the second floor, and Noah followed Emory into the kitchen. Heat radiated off him, and it was doing funny things to her insides.

"I said to split up," she whispered. She had no idea why she was whispering. Gary Poe was dead, and as far as she knew, no one else lived here. Who was going to hear them?

"I'm not leaving your side," Noah said. Doggone, the man was stubborn.

"I don't need your protection," she said airily. "I am perfectly capable of taking care of myself." She'd been doing it long enough.

"No," he agreed. "But I'm giving it to you anyway."

She gave him a long, measured look. He didn't flinch. Alrighty then.

Although the kitchen was clean and bright and well-appointed, it looked like nothing had been replaced since the house was built, sometime in the 1940s. The cupboards were definitely original, painted white to match the walls, and the tile countertops were no doubt original, too. She hoped they didn't have asbestos or lead in them.

Dishes were stacked neatly in a wire rack beside the sink. They were simple, white stoneware, not fancy or expensive. A chrome toaster, one of those cheap ones that cost ten dollars and work forever, was exactly centered on the counter against the lemon-yellow backsplash.

"Any trace of magic?" Noah asked.

It didn't quite work like that, but she didn't bother going into a long explanation. There wasn't time for it. "No sign of a spell. Likely it was done somewhere else. His workplace maybe."

A calendar hung next to the fridge. It had a fluffy kitten jumping through a field of dandelions. It was the most cheerful, personal thing she'd seen in the entire house. There were things written on some of the days. She stepped closer.

In small, neat handwriting, various appointments and reminders were printed in black ink. There was nothing written on that day's date.

Emory tapped the calendar. "No luck here. Maybe he had an appointment he didn't write down." If he had, it had to have been someplace within thirty minutes of Healing Herbs. "I wonder if there's something on his cellphone."

"Was he carrying one?"

"Not that I saw. He could have forgotten it at home." Emory had done that once or twice. "Or left it at the office."

"Or he could have dropped it on the way to your shop. Or worse, the killer could have taken it."

She sighed. "You are so negative."

He gave her a sideways look. "I prefer the term 'realistic.'"

A search of the rest of the main floor revealed nothing more interesting than that Gary Poe had been obsessively neat and possibly spent way too much time in the bathroom, if the stacks of reading material were anything to go by. There were six different magazines, ranging from fly fishing to archaeology, a joke book, three of those bizarre facts bathroom books, and a Terry Pratchett novel. At least he had good taste in fiction.

They met Edwina back in the front room.

"Any luck?" Emory asked.

She shook her head. "And his computer is gone. I'm guessing he uses a laptop, which is likely at work. No TV, either, and it doesn't look like he ever had one." She shoved her braid over one shoulder. "Who doesn't watch TV?"

"Did you find his cellphone?" Emory asked.

"No. No iPad or e-reader either. Found a stack of books and an actual boom box from the '80s. The kind that plays tapes. The guy was seriously old-school."

Which was ironic, coming from Edwina. Emory sighed. "Hopefully his laptop is at the office."

"It's almost dark," Noah pointed out. "Maybe we should try his office now."

Edwina nodded. "Emory, you can scan for spells again. He might have gotten hit with it at work."

"Just what I was thinking." Emory said.

Noah followed them out the door.

"Goddess. How are we ever going to find anything in this disaster?" Emory glanced around in horror. Gary Poe's office was the exact opposite of his home. His house was so neat it was painful, whereas his office looked like a bomb went off. "Do you suppose somebody tossed the place?"

Edwina crossed her arms and glared at the disarray as if offended by the lack of order. "Looks more like he was just messy. There's his laptop." She strode to the desk and tapped on the keyboard. "You two search the files."

Emory and Noah began pulling out drawers on the rows of filing cabinets against the west wall of Poe's private office. Noah had closed the blinds so no one would see them from the street, and the outer office was empty, everyone having cleared out shortly after closing. Hopefully it would stay that way. Emory didn't want to have to explain why she'd broken into a dead guy's office. Not that anyone else knew he was dead, but still.

Breaking in had been ridiculously easy. The locks were flimsy. Emory didn't even want to know how Noah had bypassed the alarm system.

The files were the standard stuff you'd expect to find in the office of an accountant. Blank forms, presumably for clients to fill out, hard copies of clients' personal information, and copies of the firm's tax documents. Pretty boring. Emory did find one file that sparked her interest.

"Here's a client file with a sticky note to call her today. Wilma Hacket. Maybe she's the person Gary Poe met before he came to my shop." Emory flipped through the file while Noah looked over her shoulder. She felt his warm breath on her neck, and his presence sent shivers of awareness through her. She had a hard time focusing.

"I doubt this is your woman," Noah said. "She's eighty years old."

"So what? She could still work a spell." Unlike, say, strength, stamina, or eyesight, magic grew stronger over time, which was why natural born witches like Emory and her coven lived far longer than ordinary humans. Not that she'd ever tell anyone that. It was a good way to get locked up in some secret government lab.

"She moved to Colorado last year, so she couldn't have met with him in person." He tapped the file with the woman's updated address. "Is she powerful enough to send a spell that distance?"

"If she's a witch, maybe. But that spell wasn't sent long distance." Emory was disappointed. "I'm pretty sure it was placed directly on Poe by the spell caster. Maybe through something he ate or drank. Hard to say." She stuck the file back in the drawer and continued rifling. She came up with a big, fat goose egg.

"What about you?" she asked Edwina, who was closing Gary Poe's laptop. "Were you able to get into the computer?"

"Sure. His password is 1234, if you can believe it." She grimaced as if astonished at the idiocy of some people.

"Really? Usually they want a capital letter, twelve symbols, and your first-born child," Emory said.

Noah snorted softly. She bit back a smile.

"Find anything interesting?" she asked.

"No references to anything magical or indication that he had an appointment today." She rummaged in the desk drawers. "Best bet is it's on his phone, but I'm not seeing it."

Noah was likely right. Gary had probably dropped it on his way to the herb shop, or the killer had it.

"What about the search engine?" Emory asked. "Did he look for anything interesting?"

"Sure. Lots of things. New Horizons for one."

"The drug recovery place?"

Edwina smirked. "The NASA mission. Apparently, he's a science nerd."

"Hey, don't knock nerds. What else?"

"North Head Lighthouse. Maybe he was planning a trip."

"He didn't do it today," Emory said. North Head Lighthouse was in Washington, about a two-and-a-half-hour trip. "He wouldn't have had time to drive there and back."

Edwina scrolled through more search history. "Niall Horan."

"That sounds promising," Noah said, looking up from a stack of files he was returning to their drawers.

Emory giggled. "I doubt it."

"We should follow up any leads," Noah said stiffly.

"Niall Horan is a member of One Direction." Emory tried not to giggle again.

Noah looked blank.

"It's a pop band," she explained. "Like the modern version of New Kids on the Block."

He still looked blank, which made her sputter with laughter. Edwina wasn't being so subtle. She let out a hearty guffaw.

"Never mind. It's definitely not him." Members of pop bands usually didn't go around putting magic spells on people.

"Those are the most recent searches I found," Edwina said, still clearly amused by Noah's lack of pop-culture knowledge.

Noah closed a drawer. "Then we're out of clues."

Frustration simmered. He was right. There was nowhere else to turn. For the moment, the mystery of Gary Poe's death would remain just that— a mystery.

Two days later Emory was taking her morning walk in Deepwood Park. The seventeen-acre park was crisscrossed with walking paths and dotted with towering fir trees and clusters of bright flowers. Through the trees she caught glimpses of the Willamette River as it flowed past before joining the Columbia River on its way to the Pacific Ocean.

It was a peaceful spot, popular with joggers and walkers, but it was so early, she had the place nearly to herself. A woman jogged several yards ahead of her. A flash of color in the trees parallel to the woman caught Emory's eye. Suddenly a man burst from the woods and made a flying leap at the jogger. She went down in a heap, screaming for help, clawing at the man and trying to get away. He was too strong for her though, trapping her against the ground and snarling like an animal.

For a split-second Emory was stunned, shocked into inaction by what she'd witnessed. But then she whirled into action. She ran toward the attacker, stooping to grab a stone lying next to the path. Whispering a few words over it, she heaved it at the man. It flew from her hand, faster than humanly possible, and smashed into the side of his head. He shook his head at the impact but appeared otherwise unharmed. He continued his attack.

At that moment she wished with all her might that she had been born a fire witch so she could lob a fireball at him. Or a storm witch. A shot of lightening up his backside would do the trick. In this situation, being a spellwalker was next to useless.

The man was so intent on continuing his assault, he didn't notice Emory until she roundhouse-kicked him in the face. He fell back, allowing the woman to roll away and inch painfully across the ground.

With a primal scream, the man leapt to his feet and charged, but this time his focus was on Emory. She threw up a spell so fast, she got lightheaded. The spell formed an invisible shield between the man and them. He snarled, beating his fists against a ward he couldn't see, but instead of being confused or scared, he seemed to get angrier. His eyes were bloodshot. Foam and spit flew from his mouth. It was almost as if he were rabid.

Emory pulled out her phone and dialed 911 as she squatted to check on the jogger. She had a couple of bruises blossoming but otherwise seemed fine. Emory told the operator where they were and what was happening. "Hurry. This guy is nuts. I don't know how long we can avoid him. If he gets his hands on us, we're as good as dead." A slight exaggeration, perhaps, but she wasn't willing to risk either of their lives.

She hung up. She didn't have time to stay on the line and answer questions. The shield was temporary, and it was already failing.

She threw out another spell to strengthen it, but the continuous bashing was a major energy drain. She was already exhausted. "Hold on," she whispered to the woman, squeezing her shoulder gently. "Help is coming."

The woman whimpered, her eyes fixed on the crazy man, clearly confused about what was happening.

The shield was weakening with each bash from the attacker's fists, but Emory also heard the wail of sirens as police cars poured into the parking lot on the hill above. Blue uniforms appeared through the trees, running toward the scene. She let the shield fall.

The man flew at Emory, tackling her and driving them both to the ground. The air whooshed out of her lungs, leaving her gasping for breath like a fish out of water. She threw out a mental spell, and it punched him in the face. He reared back, the moment of distraction enough for her to get her breath back. She punched and twisted and scratched, trying to unseat him or at least hold him off until the cops got there.

A brawny policeman grabbed the man under the armpits and hauled him off her. The guy whirled and threw a punch at the officer, howling like a freaking werewolf while he did it. Except he wasn't a were. Emory was sure of it. He wasn't anything magical.

"Need some help here," the cop shouted.

A woman half his size ran up and grabbed the attacker's arm, wrenching it behind him and forcing him to the ground. The attacker howled again and threw her several feet. A third police officer appeared with what looked like a gun in his hand. He pulled the trigger and several wires snaked out. It took three jolts of electricity to bring him down so he could be handcuffed and carted away when the ambulance arrived.

While the police dealt with him, and the EMTs attended the victim, Emory threw up a camouflage spell and slipped away without anyone noticing. It was never a good idea for a witch to get involved with the authorities, even here in Deepwood. They had what they needed. They did not need her. Thanks to the spell, they'd never remember she was there.

What she needed right now was donuts, and lots of them.

CHAPTER
NINE

"Oh my goddess, are you okay?" Lene asked as Emory approached the shop carrying a large pink box. She plucked a twig out of Emory's hair.

"I'm fine. You should see the other guy." She laughed lightly and unlocked the shop door. "You're here early." Lene typically didn't open her bookstore until a good hour after Healing Herbs.

Lene sniffed the box. "The donuts called to me I guess."

Emory plopped the donut box on the counter, flipped it open, and plucked out a blueberry cake donut, biting into it with a happy sigh. Virgil never let her down.

From his cage, Fred gave an aggravated squeak. He was probably picking up on her anxiety.

Lene selected a Bavarian cream and eyed Emory. "What happened?" She took a huge bite.

"What makes you think something happened?"

"Please. You came in carrying enough donuts to feet a football team." Her voice came out muffled around the mouth full of donut.

That was the problem with best friends. They knew you too well.

Emory told her about the crazed man in the park. "It was so weird. Like he was on drugs or something. Maybe those bath salts things they're always talking about on the news. He acted like a moon-crazed werewolf, but he was definitely human."

"That's strange," Lene said. "I was reading online this morning that some woman attacked another woman in the mall in Moreland yesterday. Same sort of thing. Bloodshot eyes, foaming at the mouth, crazy insane strength, screaming like an animal. They said it was the third assault this month. Do you think there's a rabies epidemic?"

"The guy did look like a rabid dog, but I don't think that's it. I have a bad feeling there's something else going on. I just can't put my finger on it." She shook her head. "Nothing we can do about it, though."

"I suppose not. How'd the date with Noah go?" She smirked.

"Don't be ridiculous. It wasn't a date. It was an investigation, and Edwina was there."

"That does put a damper on things."

There was a tinkle from the door, and Veri sauntered in. "How was your date with my cousin?" she asked, propping one hip against the counter. She was wearing a tight, black and red dress that hit mid-thigh and showed off a whole lot of curvy leg and lipstick-red heels to match. Gold jewelry popped against her dark skin. Her hair was down in soft, brown waves, and she'd done some sort of Cleopatra thing with her eyes. Emory figured she was probably the one with the date.

"It wasn't a date," she repeated, offering Veri a donut. She took a coconut one.

"Sure it wasn't." Veri picked up a vanilla and fig candle and sniffed it before putting it back down. She munched happily on her donut, in no hurry to return to her shop; she wasn't going anywhere until Emory spilled the beans.

"We were trying to find information on Gary Poe's death." Emory opened a box of spices while alternatively nibbling on her donut. She'd recently decided to expand the shop's repertoire. Many spices had healing properties. Why not use them?

"If you say so. What happened? Did you find out anything about the dead guy?"

"Not much. Nothing that would lead us to the killer. We're back to square one, I'm afraid."

"That's too bad," Lene said. "I'm certain he was a nice man. The dead guy, I mean, not the killer."

Emory gave her a look. How Lene knew that was beyond her, but Lene thought the best of people.

"How's Mia?" Lene gave Emory a casual look as she changed subjects, but Emory knew the question was anything but.

"I talked to her yesterday. Well, texted actually. She's not much for talking on the phone. She's got a major chip on her shoulder, but I think we can help her," Emory said.

"Of course we can, but should we?" Veri asked. She tapped one long, turquoise nail on the counter. Veri was never comfortable letting others in on their inner circle workings. She liked to keep things mysterious. Except, apparently, for her cousin, Noah.

"Of course we should," Lene said.

"We'll go slowly," Emory agreed, "but I think it's important to help her. I have a feeling she might be one of us."

"Duh. We know she's a witch," Veri said, rooting around in the pink box for another donut.

"Not the witch thing," Emory said. "The other thing."

"A portal guardian?" whispered Lene, glancing around as if to make sure no one overheard though the shop was empty except for the three of them.

"Is that even possible?" Veri asked shakily, a raspberry cream halfway to her lips. "I thought we were the last."

And there it was. The thing that had drawn them all together. Their blood. Their destiny. The last of the portal witches.

There were, those among the witchborn who belonged to an ancient bloodline stretching back millennia. A single coven had been chosen to protect the portal system that spanned the worlds between worlds. It was the system Emory had used to send Edwina, Noah, and herself to the bayou to hide Gary Poe's body. She was one of that bloodline, as were Veri and Lene.

Once upon a time, there had been many hundreds of decedents of the original witches, capable of controlling the powerful pathways of the portal system. But during the witch hunts of the fifteenth through eighteen centuries, most of them had been annihilated and much of the knowledge of the portals lost. To find three witches of that bloodline was a miracle. To discover a fourth would be akin to finding a unicorn.

"What if she's one of the dark ones?" Veri said, practical to the point of negativity. There were those who sought to use the portal ways for their own gain.

"That's why we go slowly. We help her, but we stay vigilant. We watch. We test her. We'll know." Emory had no doubt of that. "We're all agreed?"

They gave her the thumbs-up. Although Emory was head of the coven, her word was not law. The coven was a true democracy. That was how witches did things. The good ones, anyway.

"I think we should have a coven meeting," Veri suggested. "It's a good moon phase, and it wouldn't be a bad idea to consult the goddess on a few things."

Emory agreed. "Tonight at my house. Just after dark."

"I better go open up the shop," Veri said. She paused at the door. "By the way, did you hear about that crazy woman at the mall? Third one this month. People are losing their minds, I tell you." With a shake of her head, she sashayed out the door.

"Girl," Emory said softly. "You have no idea."

"I'm pretty sure most covens don't bake chocolate chip cookies as a means to connect with the wisdom of the universe," Lene said drily as she stirred a cup of semi-sweet chocolate chips into dough.

"Well maybe they should," Veri said, swiping a spoonful of dough and popping it in her mouth. She gave a small moan. "Sure is tastier than bat wings and toads' eyes."

Emory snorted. "You know very well that magic is stronger when worked on a full stomach, and there's nothing better to fill the stomach than chocolate chip cookies."

"Hear, hear!" Veri raised her glass of wine in a toast.

Fred was wide awake and perched on the flour jar, nose twitching. He very obviously wanted cookie dough, and he very definitely wasn't getting any.

Veri ignored Lene. "This dough tastes different than usual."

"That's because I put a spell on it," Emory said, sliding the first batch of cookies in the oven. She turned to find the other two staring at her in horror. She burst out laughing. "What? You think I'm going to turn you into newts or something? You should see the looks on your faces!" She doubled over with giggles.

"Very funny," Lene said drily. "Now what did you do to our cookies?"

Emory held up her hands as if to fend off their glares. "I bespelled the vanilla with a little love magic. Vanilla is an excellent magical ingredient for attracting love."

Lene and Veri exchanged glances. "You what now?" Lene asked.

"You dosed us with a love potion?" Veri asked.

"Of course not. It's just an attraction spell to draw love of all sorts—not just romance—to us. We could use a little more of it around here, don't you think?" Emory said, dropping dough on a baking sheet. "Especially with all the death and craziness going on."

"I get you," Veri finally said. "But what else did you do to it?"

Emory smiled. They knew her too well. "I put in a tiny bit of black pepper for protection."

They stared at the bowl of dough. "You put pepper in our cookies? How could you do that?" Veri sounded horrified. "That's like adding finger paint to the Mona Lisa."

Fred chittered as if to agree. Emory shot him a look. *What do you know about cookies?*

Lene swiped more of the dough. "Stop whining. You can hardly taste it. Besides, Emory is right. We need protection, and a little love wouldn't be a bad idea. I, for one, am all for it. Bring on the hotties!"

Veri gave up. "Fine. Whatevs. Now what are we going to do about that girl?"

Emory knew exactly who she meant. "I think we need to look a little deeper into Mia's background. She seemed very freaked out by her visions. I don't think she was raised properly as a witch."

Lene frowned. "You think somebody hid it from her?"

"That, or whoever raised her didn't know either." Emory remembered what Mia had said about her mother. "Or maybe they died before they could pass on the knowledge."

"We should test her." Veri took a long swig of wine as Emory removed the cookies from the oven. "She might not be one of us, you know. She could just be an ordinary witch. Or not a witch at all. She could be part Sidhe or something. You're just guessing she has anything to do with the portals."

Emory *was* guessing, but she'd sensed something in Mia the others hadn't. It went deep, too. Beyond magic. Emory was certain they were connected.

She transferred cookies to the cooling rack, although at the rate Veri was going, they wouldn't have time to cool. "We test Mia. Find out exactly what she is. Maybe see if we can figure out how her visions work. One way or another, this girl needs our help and we need hers. Agreed?"

"Agreed," the other two chorused around mouths full of warm cookies.

"But we should deal with the dead man first," Lene pointed out. "That's priority number one."

"Yes," Emory said. "Once the investigation is complete, we'll start testing Mia."

"Speaking of the dead man: what about him and all the other weird stuff that's been going on?" Veri asked.

Emory sighed. "I have no idea. I've gone about as far as I can go with the investigation into Gary Poe's murder at the moment. Unless we stumble randomly across some clue, I don't see what else we can do. As for the other weirdness... all those people attacking each other? I don't see what that has to do with us or how we can stop it."

"Probably bad pharmaceuticals," Lene said darkly, taking another cookie. "Have you seen what that stuff can do to people?" Emory and Veri ignored her. Lene had a fondness for conspiracy theories. This week it was bad pharma. Next week it would be Ancient Astronauts or Area 51 cover-ups.

"We could invite Edwina over and see if she can sense something," Emory suggested.

"What, have her channel Poe's spirit?" Veri asked. "That's more Lene's thing."

"I'm not channeling anyone's spirit," Lene snapped, refilling her wine glass.

"No one's asking you to." Emory rescued another batch of cookies from the oven before switching off the heat. "Edwina is a sensitive though. She can sometimes sense things if we get her in the right mood. It might be our best bet."

Veri shrugged and poured herself more wine. "Sure. Why not? Can she come over tonight?"

Emory glanced at the clock. It was late, but Edwina sometimes kept strange hours. She sent a text and got one back almost immediately.

"Norma's is open late tonight." In addition to serving the best pie in the state, possibly the entire country, Edwina read the tarot for special customers. "She said she can come tomorrow if that works for us."

They nodded, so Emory set it up. She felt better once things were arranged, like they were doing something rather than sitting around waiting. For what, she wasn't sure.

The meeting was just breaking up when there was a pounding on the door. Emory went to open it. Noah was on the other side.

"Are you here to pick up Veri?" she asked, surprised to see him. She was certain Veri had driven her own car.

"Noah, what the heck?" Veri snapped, moving in behind her. "Are you following me?"

He didn't even look at her. He was focused on Emory. "I need you."

Her heart fluttered in her throat, and her stomach started doing a tango with her spleen.. "What?" she managed to squeak.

His expression was grim. "I found another body."

Potions, Poisons and Peril

CHAPTER
TEN

"Why didn't you call the police? This is sort of their job." Emory clung desperately to the handle above the door as the jeep zipped around a corner. She'd never been so glad in her life for the invention of seatbelts.

"Because the police aren't spellwalkers," Noah said, taking another corner at full tilt.

Dread pooled in her stomach. He wanted her to walk a spell surrounding a dead person. "We should notify... somebody." She gritted her teeth as he tailgated the car in front of them for about a block before whipping around it with a screech of tires.

"We will. After you spellwalk the scene."

"Who died and made you the king of Deepwood?"

He didn't even crack a smile. What was up with this guy?

He pulled up in front of a brick apartment building that had probably been built circa 1910. It was the kind of place that had creaky wood floors, claw foot tubs, and old-fashioned radiators that steamed up the windows. In other words, it had atmosphere.

Noah pulled a key out of his pocket and let himself into the building. He took the stairs two at a time while Emory climbed at a more sedate pace. If the victim was dead, rushing around like a crazy person wasn't going to help.

"Hurry up," he snapped. "The spell might dissipate."

Well, there was that. How did he know so much about spells?

On the third floor, Noah pushed the fire door open onto a dimly lit hall. There were doors on either side of the hall, each clearly marked with elegant brass numbers. Four on the right, three on the left. He led her to the last door on the right and let them in.

The stink of stale beer and death hit Emory hard. She gagged a little before stiffening her spine. *I can do this.* But goddess, she'd love to have a bottle of peppermint oil on hand right about now.

The apartment was a small studio with a Murphy bed against one wall and a tiny bistro table shoved under the only window. A single blue lounge chair that had seen better days was placed in front of an impressive flat-screen television hooked up to three different gaming systems. The rest of the room was bare. Emory saw a miniscule kitchenette through an open doorway. Doors with glass knobs led to what she assumed were the bathroom and closet.

In the middle of the room, halfway between the kitchen and lounge chair, sprawled the body of a man face-down. A can of cheap beer lay on its side a few inches from his outstretched hand, a sticky, a brown puddle around it.

"How the Hades did you find the guy all the way up here?" She doubted he'd stumbled across him randomly.

"Mitch Kerrigan is—was—a friend. I came to check on him."

"I'm so sorry." Emory reached over to squeeze his arm, but he held himself so stiffly, she wasn't sure her sympathy was appreciated. She stepped closer to the body. There was scarring up one arm. It was bad. She'd seen something like that before, usually on the news, but sometimes veterans sought out her expertise with herbal remedies, although it was rarely the physical scars they wanted her to heal. There was no doubt in her mind the scars on the man in front of her were shrapnel wounds. "He was in the army with you."

If Noah was surprised, he didn't show it. "Yes."

She didn't express her sympathy again, but her heart went out to him. There was nothing as painful as losing a brother or sister in arms. Those of witchblood were bonded on a level that went far deeper than that of family or friendship. When one of them was lost, all of them suffered.

"There's definitely a spell at work here."

She knelt beside the body, closed her eyes, and drew a deep breath. Focusing her energy, she opened her inner vision. Symbols danced above the victim. Already they were beginning to dissipate.

"This spell is the same one that was put on Gary Poe. Same colors, everything." She frowned as one particular symbol stood out, or rather a partial symbol. She'd seen the same thing at Poe's scene, but it was fading too fast to make out clearly.

"Same killer?"

"Quite likely, yes. The essence is the same." She allowed him to help her up. "Was your friend of the, ah,

97

magical persuasion?" Surely it was safe to ask. He knew about Veri and the rest of them, after all.

"Mitch? I have no idea. Anything is possible."

She pondered for a moment. "It would be good to know."

"Was the killer here?"

"Probably not. I think the spell was cast somewhere else, like with Poe, though nearby. We should search the place. Maybe there's a clue to what happened. I'll take the bathroom."

He strode toward the kitchen. She was about half a step away from the bathroom when the door flew open, practically bashing her in the forehead. Someone sprang out so fast all she caught was a blur as the person, dressed in a dark sweatshirt with the hood up, threw her to the floor and took off to the door. She hit hard, pain lancing her left arm.

"Noah!"

He ran from the kitchen, took in the situation, and raced after the intruder. Footsteps pounded down the hall, but there were no shouts. A door slammed once, then again. Then silence.

She got to her feet, wincing as she jarred her arm. She really hoped it wasn't broken. Spending the evening in the ER was not her idea of fun. She closed her eyes and did a quick internal scan, one of the perks of her abilities. She couldn't psychically scan anyone else, but she could assess herself for injury and illness to some degree.

Not broken, but badly bruised and strained. She was going to need to ice it and maybe dose herself with white willow bark when she got home.

Keeping the arm clamped tightly to her side, she went into the bathroom. She was convinced the intruder was the killer or related to Mitch's death. Why else would he or she be hiding in the victim's bathroom? She couldn't say for certain, of course. She hadn't had time to scan them for spellwork residue. It had all happened too quickly for her to focus her abilities.

The bathroom yielded nothing, nor did the kitchen, except for a wall calendar of hot-rods, the current month ripped off. Had there been something on the calendar the killer didn't want them to see?

She jacked up her senses, looking for magical residue. She caught the faintest trace of it on a mug next to the sink. It was still wet, as if it had been recently rinsed out. She sniffed, hoping to catch a trace of the drink. She was pretty sure it was tea, although Mitch didn't seem like the tea-drinking kind. There was no tea bag or leaves, not even in the garbage, and there was no sink disposal. The intruder must have taken it with them.

"Emory?"

"In here." She poked her head out of the kitchen as Noah re-entered the apartment.

"No luck, huh?"

He shook his head. "Slippery bastard. Had a car waiting. License plate was covered. You?"

"I'm pretty sure the spell was placed on some tea."

He frowned. "I wouldn't have figured Mitch for a tea drinker."

"That's what I thought, too." She glanced at the body.

"This helps, though. We can trace the tea, right?"

"The killer took it with him. There is no way to trace what kind of tea it was, never mind where Mitch got it."

He let out a string of expletives.

"Exactly."

"Did you finish searching?"

"Just the kitchen and bathroom."

"I'll get the closet if you check out here."

She prowled the main room. Nothing spoke to her, so she impulsively tipped up the lounge chair. Her grandfather had had one of these. Things were always either getting kicked underneath them or falling through the cracks between the seat cushion and the frame, collecting beneath it like a graveyard of lost items.

She winced as pain shot up her arm. Maybe she shouldn't have done that, but a flash of bright color caught her attention. She toed it out from under the chair. It was a fluorescent orange Post-it. She picked it up. Something was scrawled across it in black ink: *11a.m. Friday.*

"Noah, I found something."

It looked like a fairly new Post-it. The intruder must have missed it.

"Let me see." He held out his hand, and she passed it over.

"Friday was yesterday," she mused. "And 11:00 a.m. was a few hours before Gary Poe died. Kind of a coincidence, don't you think?"

He handed it back. "Bit of a stretch. That could have been under the chair for weeks, and it could be any Friday."

"Maybe, but I have a strong feeling these deaths are connected."

Noah gently rolled Mitch's body into the grave. Mitch hadn't had much in the way of family or friends and had cut himself off from everyone after coming back from Afghanistan. Only Noah had bothered to keep in touch, never giving up on his Army buddy. And now Mitch was gone. No more beer over baseball games. No more silent comradery. He felt...hollow.

Emory had wanted to call the police, but he had refused. There was no one but him to report Mitch missing. No one but him to mourn.

She had opened another portal, and they'd spent the last couple of hours digging into the soft ground next to where they'd buried Gary Poe. It seemed wrong to bury Mitch in the middle of a swamp, where no one would ever find his grave. The man had fought for his country. He'd been a hero. But Noah knew there wasn't another way. The police couldn't be involved in this. Besides, Mitch would have hated being laid out on a slab. He'd have actually liked it out here in the middle of nowhere.

"You want to say some words?" Emory asked.

Noah swallowed. Did he? He'd buried far more friends than there were words. He shook his head and shoveled dirt on top the man who'd been his friend. After it was done, he stood for a long moment to honor the fallen hero. When Emory wasn't looking, he made a sign above the grave. It was a magical sigil he'd learned long ago. It meant "rest in peace, go with the gods, live again."

She took his hand as they walked back to the portal. It was nice having someone touch him just for comfort. No demands, no expectations.

He followed her through the portal, and it occurred to him he'd follow her anywhere.

Potions, Poisons and Peril

CHAPTER
ELEVEN

Next to Saturdays, Sundays were the busiest day for Healing Herbs. Emory opened at noon when the church people were leaving services and headed to the nearest restaurant for a bite. It was amazing how many church people ended up inside her shop, buying herbal remedies for everything from hangnails to straying husbands.

Fred had been quiet in his cage all day, only coming out for the occasional snack. Still, it was comforting to have him near.

She felt bad for Noah. It would be hard to deal with the death of a friend, especially when it had happened in such a bizarre way. And then having to hide it from the authorities.

It was nearly five, and the shop was empty when Noah strolled in. Emory hadn't expected to see him, so it was a pleasant surprise. She felt that fizz of attraction sizzling through her.

"Hi, Noah. How are you?" He'd stoically handled last night without batting an eyelash. Maybe it was an army thing.

"Better now."

"Good. Can I help you with something?"

"I wanted to see if you were free for dinner."

She was stunned. He was asking her out? Or was he? Maybe this was just a friend thing. Like supernatural community bonding or something.

She opened her mouth, not sure how she was going to answer, and the doorbell jangled. A middle-aged woman pushed her way in. She was a little on the plump side and was wearing a teal-and-white polka-dot dress that hit mid-calf. Her feet were shod in sensible black patent-leather pumps with modest, one-inch heels. Her purse, clutched tightly in work-worn hands, matched her shoes. She screamed "church lady."

"Excuse me," Emory murmured to Noah, moving toward the newcomer. Church Lady looked nervous. "Welcome." Emory shot her a warm smile, hoping to ease her nerves. "May I help you with something?"

Her eyes, the skin beneath them so dark as to seem almost bruised, darted to Noah. "I don't know..."

Emory steered her gently toward the alcove. "Why don't we have a cup of tea and talk about it over here, where we won't be interrupted."

Church Lady sat on the chair facing the front of the store. She kept her purse on her lap, gripping it like a security blanket.

"I'll be right back with tea." Emory paused by Noah. "Would you mind watching the shop for a bit?" She said it loud enough that her visitor would hear. Emory didn't want her thinking they were conspiring or something.

"Of course. Shall I close at five if you're not done?"

"Yes, please. Thank you." She squeezed his arm before hurrying to the back room. The kettle was still warm, so it didn't take long to throw together a tea tray. She breathed a sigh of relief to find her visitor still sitting ramrod straight in the alcove.

She always wondered why people who were so anti-witch would take up residence in a town dedicated to witches. It took all types, she supposed.

Placing the tray on the coffee table, Emory offered Church Lady a cup. She sniffed at it before taking a careful sip. She made a slight face and reached for the sugar. Three lumps later she tried again. This time, no face.

"Like it?" Emory asked, taking a seat.

"It's okay." She sipped again. A good sign. That particular blend was meant to sooth and calm. Church Lady looked like she needed all the help she could get in that department.

"My name is Emory Chastain." She lifted her cup, waiting.

The woman wasn't supernatural, and she didn't seem the type to seek out help from an herbalist or a spellwalker, so she must really be at her wits' end.

Church Lady set the cup down carefully on the table. "Susan. My name is Susan."

"I assume someone referred you to me?"

"Yes. A woman named Edwina. I met her at the grocery store. She told me you could help me with my problem."

Interesting. Didn't the church frown on tarot readings and energy crystals? Although maybe that was excusable if one made really excellent pie, like Edwina.

"What sort of problem?"

Susan leaned forward, her expression grim. "I think someone put a spell on my husband."

"What makes you think that?"

"We've been married ten years. Mostly good. But lately he's changed."

"Changed how?" Emory took a sip of her tea. It could use a bit more honey.

"He's become... not very nice."

Emory frowned. "How so?"

"He says mean things to me. Yells a lot."

"Does he hit you?"

She seemed appalled at the idea. "Oh, no. Well, not yet. He just threatens."

Susan's husband sounded like an abusive jerk, but Emory couldn't take the risk magic wasn't involved. "I would like to meet him."

Susan paled. "Why?"

"To verify he's under a spell."

"He must be," she said emphatically. "It's that or he's possessed by demons. Why else would he change like that?"

Emory could think of several reasons: stress, drugs, alcohol, an affair—none of which she planned to mention to Susan. No sense ruffling feathers unless absolutely necessary. "I'll need to figure out what kind of spell he's under if I'm going to break it. Or free him of the demon, if that's the case." She tried really hard to keep a straight face. Despite popular belief, demons were corporeal and therefore couldn't go around possessing people.

"Oh." Susan thought it over. "That makes sense."

"Is there a time or place where I can meet him? Discreetly, of course. So I can assess the situation."

Susan glanced at her watch. "I'm supposed to meet him at Wyld Oats in fifteen minutes to do our weekly shopping."

Wyld Oats was just a few blocks away at the end of Main Street. It was a combination health food store and regular grocery, with a mixture of locally sourced, organic items and big-name mainstream brands. It was Emory's favorite place to shop, especially the cheese section. Each week she'd pick out a new one to try, from Pierre Robert triple-creme to nutty, tangy Red Leicester. She might have a cheese addiction.

"Perfect. I'm about to close up, so I'll head down there."

Susan frowned. "Will you be able to assess him inside the store? Because he'll get real mad if he figures it out."

She squeezed her hand. "Don't worry. Everything will be fine."

Susan stood. "All right, then. I'll see you there. What about the results?"

"Come back Tuesday, and we can discuss what I find."

"All right. Thank you," Susan said stiffly. She rose, spun on her heel, and strode from the store as if the hounds of hell were nipping at her feet. Maybe they were. Emory doubted her faith was keen on cavorting with witches.

"You're not going there alone," Noah said.

"Oh, yes I am. I do this all the time. It's part of my job."

"It might be dangerous."

"It might, but I've learned to take care of myself. Besides"—she looked him up and down— "you'd stick out like a sore thumb. I don't need you glaring at everybody and freaking out the shoppers."

"Then I'll wait in the car."

"Seriously, Noah, I do not need a babysitter."

"I didn't think you did."

She glared at him. "Why do you want to go, then?"

"Because it'll make me feel better. If you do get into more trouble than you can handle, think of me as backup. I'll take you out to dinner afterward."

She mulled it over. It was true she had no idea what Susan's husband was like. She doubted he'd go off in the middle of a grocery store, but you never knew. And dinner after would be good. They could talk about… things. And she'd need some fortification for the coven meeting that night.

"Okay, but you stay in the car and don't come in unless I call you."

"Deal."

Wyld Oats was surprisingly busy for a Sunday evening. She didn't want to look suspicious, so she took one of the mini carts and wheeled it slowly around the store. She threw in a box of pasta and a jar of sauce with a cute label, then pretended to look at the nutritional content of various items until she spotted Susan and her husband. It didn't take long. The store wasn't that big. They were in the cereal aisle, and Mr. Susan was currently berating his wife for not selecting the right brand.

"You're so stupid," he snarled, grabbing a box from the cart and slamming it back on the shelf so hard, it crumpled. "Can't you do anything right?" He snatched some kind of sugar cereal and dumped it in the cart.

"But I like that cereal." Her voice was pitched so low, Emory could barely hear her. Susan didn't look at her husband, instead keeping her eyes on the floor.

"Who cares, you stupid cow! You're too fat anyway. You don't need cereal." There were a lot of additional expletives to his diatribe.

Her blood began to boil, but she kept a lid on her temper. If this was a spell, it wasn't his fault. If it wasn't a spell, he was an abusive jerk, and she might just put one on him, consequences be hanged.

She picked up a box of wheat squares and pretended to read the label while she scanned him for signs of magical tampering. There were none. Mr. Susan's aura was angry red and black and muddy brown, with tinges of bilious yellow-green. Ugly, just like him.

Placing the box in her cart, she calmly wheeled her way past the couple. Neither of them looked at her, Susan because she didn't want to give anything away, and Mr. Susan because he was too busy berating his wife. She scanned him again, but there was nothing. Mr. Susan was just a full-on prick.

She turned the corner and went to the front of the store. She left the cart, items and all, and exited to the parking lot. Noah was waiting right where she'd left him, thrumming his fingers against the steering wheel as if she'd taken hours instead of minutes.

"So?" he asked when she slid into the seat next to him.

"Nothing."

"No spell?"

"Nope. Just a big, fat jerk."

"I could beat some sense into him," he offered.

She smiled. "That's sweet of you, but we're going to have to let Susan deal with this. I'll give her the tools, but she's going to have to make her own decision. That's how these things work."

He muttered something under his breath but didn't argue. He started the car and pulled out of the parking lot.

"Where are we going?" she asked.

A tiny smile quirked his mouth. "Someplace very special."

Well, wasn't that mysterious.

CHAPTER

TWELVE

"Someplace very special" turned out to be Cartlandia, a popular food truck gathering place in a disused parking lot next to the town hall. She'd been there a few times and loved that she could get everything from gluten-free crepes to sinfully rich lobster wraps. For dessert there was always the bright yellow cart that sold individual sweet potato pies spiked with rum. Still, it wasn't exactly what she would call "special."

Noah led her through the hodgepodge of cars, the scents of the food on offer perfuming the air, to the very back. One seller was off by himself, as if everyone had forgotten he was there.

It was an old-fashioned Airstream with aluminum sides and curved roof. An A-frame sign out front declared it had the best Polynesian food this side of the Pacific. A single unoccupied picnic table was placed under a blue-and-white striped awning. Not exactly what Emory had expected for a first date. At least it would be quick, and she could get back in time for the coven meeting.

A head popped out through the window and a round face beamed at them. "What's up, brutha?" shouted the exceedingly large man inside. He wore a loud Hawaiian shirt covered in hibiscus flowers, and his tawny brown skin was beaded with sweat.

"Nothin' much. Good to see ya." Noah did a weird fist bump thing with the guy.

"What can I get ya?" the man asked, tossing a grin at Emory as he mopped his forehead with a white towel.

"A plate of your finest," Noah said with a grin. Both of them looked expectantly at Emory.

There was no menu, so Emory was baffled. How could she order if she didn't know what they served? "I'll have what he's having," she said, jerking her thumb at Noah.

"Good choice. Good choice. Have a seat, and I'll bring it right out." The big man disappeared inside and Emory heard the distinctive sounds of food preparation.

Noah guided her to the picnic bench. They sat down across from each other. He seemed more at ease than she'd ever seen him. Almost content.

"So, the cook. You know him?"

"Aulii? We go way back." He smiled as if the thought brought up pleasant memories.

She eyed him. "How far?"

"Pretty far." He paused. "Since we were kids."

It was the first hint he'd given about his past. He'd grown up with a future Polynesian cook and food cart owner.

"Aulii is an unusual name. Sounds Hawaiian."

"Something like that."

Goddess above, it was like pulling teeth. "It's good you're still friends." She had few connections left to her own past. Lene was one. Her aunt, Lily was the other, and Lily was off enjoying retirement in Colorado, of all places.

Noah nodded but didn't say anything. They sat for a moment in awkward silence that was broken when Aulii stomped out of the trailer, two massive plates of food in his hands.

"Here ya go." He slapped them down. "Best Polynesian this side of the Pacific." He beamed. "Enjoy." Then he turned around and hoisted himself back into the small trailer.

Emory stared at her plate, eyes wide. It was a massive portion of rice, noodles, veggies, meats, and goodness knew what else, all smothered in some kind of sauce. It was enough to feed a small army.

"Wow. This is... a lot."

He said nothing. He just dug in, enjoyment written all over his face. If he liked it that much, it must be good. She loaded her fork, popped it in her mouth and chewed. Explosions of flavor danced across her tongue. She'd had Hawaiian before, but this was nothing like it. In fact, it was like nothing she'd ever tasted. The sauce was rich, tangy, with a hint of something she couldn't quite place. The veggies were mostly identifiable, but there were a couple she had no idea about. They were crunchy and slightly sweet, and she wanted to gobble them down like a crazy person. Must be imported.

"Oh my goddess, this is so good," she mumbled around a mouthful of the spicy stuff.

"You like it?"

"Oh, gods, yes." Then she couldn't talk because her mouth was too full.

"It's my favorite cuisine, bar none," he said. Another reveal, small though it was.

"I can see why," she said once her mouth was empty. She forked up another big bite. "Aulii is a genius."

He laughed. "I'll tell him you said that. I'm sure he'll be pleased."

They fell into silence, and she searched for something to talk about. "Did you grow up in New Orleans?"

He blinked, confused. "New Orleans?"

"Veri is from New Orleans, so I just assumed, you being cousins and all."

"I grew up in a lot of places. We moved around a lot."

"Oh, was your mom or dad in the military?"

"Military. Yes. My dad."

"So you followed in his footsteps."

His eyes took on a faraway look. "I guess I did. Military was always sort of a family business."

Odd. She'd never heard Veri mention any relatives in the military, but she hadn't known Veri that long. "I guess that explains how you met Aulii."

He seemed oddly relieved. "Exactly. How about you? Where'd you grow up?"

"Seattle," she said. "Or rather a small town just outside it. My family wasn't terribly popular with the locals, as you can imagine. We were too different."

"They knew you were witches?"

"They accused us of being witches. They didn't really *know*. It's kind of a long story." And ugly. She didn't want to go into it.

"I've got time." He propped his elbows on the table.

"But I don't. I'm supposed to be meeting the coven. Edwina's coming over, and we're going to try and figure out what's going on psychically. You know, with Gary Poe and your buddy, Mitch."

Noah's expression turned stark, and she regretted her words instantly. "Where are you meeting? I can drive you."

"My house. You can come too, if you like," she said impulsively.

He nodded. "I'd like that, and on our way, you can tell me this long story of yours."

Darn. So she wasn't getting out of it. "All right."

They said a quick goodbye to Aulii, who made Emory promise to come back, then climbed in Noah's jeep and headed toward Emory's house.

"So the neighbors thought you were witches," he prompted when she didn't immediately start talking.

"The story isn't a pretty one."

"Doesn't have to be. It's your story." He made it sound as if the mere act of being her story made it the most important thing in the world. She couldn't help but feel warm and gooey inside.

"My mother and grandparents moved to Port Arton in Washington shortly before I was born. The town they'd lived in before became a little too hot for those with supernatural abilities."

"Your father?"

She shrugged. "Never knew him, but that was fine because my grandfather filled that role. Everything went well at first, then my mother began dating one of the local men."

"This was a problem?"

"To the women it was. We were outsiders. Odd. Different. She was taking one of their men, so they decided to do something about it."

"Crap," he muttered under his breath.

She gave a grim smile. "Indeed. The good citizens of Port Arton were used to us being a little strange. Not going to church, doing weird things in the moonlight, celebrating odd holidays. But this? Dating one of them? This took their

115

suspicions into overdrive. Somebody started muttering about witchcraft and Satanism. There was a contingent of 'good church people,' who decided they were going to do something about the evil in their midst. They arrested and tried my mother for a crime she didn't commit."

He gave her a steady look. "There's more, isn't there?"

"Yes," she said softly. "The man she was dating, the one who'd claimed to love her, didn't just abandon her. He testified against her. He was the star witness. It was all nonsense, of course, but the jury bought it hook, line, and sinker."

"Idiots."

"Oh, it gets better. The man was a supernatural, like us. He was witchblood. But he sold my mother out to save his own skin so the townspeople wouldn't suspect the truth about him. After the trial, he disappeared."

"Oh, gods of the sea, Emory, I am so sorry."

He looked genuinely upset.

"It was a long time ago," she assured him.

He took her hand, linking his fingers with hers. A thrum of warm energy pulsed from where their fingers touched through her entire body. Suddenly she was in dire need of a frosty beverage. Or a cold shower.

"It must have been so painful for you. Especially with the double betrayal."

"It was, but time has a way of healing old wounds. Although believe me, I will never trust another witchblood man again."

For a moment it was as if he'd been turned to stone. Then he gave a strained smile. She winced, suddenly realizing what he must think. He was Veri's kin, which meant he might be witchblood, too.

116

Before she could apologize or explain, he said, "I assume they put your mother in jail?"

"Worse. They tortured her. They claimed they were helping her, that she was crazy and needed specialized treatment. More like 'casting out demons' or something stupid. In reality, it was torture. They locked her up in an asylum. Filled her with drugs and zapped her with electricity until she drooled. And that's where she stayed until the day she died."

He squeezed her hand. His skin was warm while hers was suddenly cold. His presence was a soothing balm to the harsh memories.

"My grandparents were afraid I'd be next. That the witch would betray the rest of us as well, so to keep me safe, they sent me to Deepwood to live with my aunt Lily a while. That's when I met Lene. Lily helped me learn to control my abilities and taught me herb lore. After my grandfather passed away, grandmother returned, and we moved to Seattle. She's the one who taught me what it was to be a portal witch."

"Your mother?" he asked softly.

"She died when I was twenty-four. Buried in a pauper's grave." Because grandmother had been gone by then, and she'd been too afraid to claim her mother's body lest they discover her power and lock her up, too.

"I'm so sorry." He traced gentle circles on the back of her hand. "How did she die?"

"They claimed it was natural. Heart attack. But my mother was still young and a witch to boot. We don't generally drop dead of heart attacks."

"You think she was killed?"

"That or an accident. It was definitely the result of their torture. They called it pretty names like 'hydrotherapy' and 'electrical therapy,' but you can guess what was really happening."

"I'm surprised they would allow that sort of thing, what, twenty years ago? That's some serious old-school stuff."

She snorted. Aw, wasn't he sweet. "Noah, I'm a witch."

He gave her a baffled look. "So?"

"Surely you know witches live longer than ordinary humans."

"Veri might have said something about that, but it never really registered. What does that have to do with anything?"

"This was closer to a hundred years ago."

His eyes widened. "I know it's impolite to ask a lady her age…."

She laughed. "Technically, I'm ninety-three." How was he going to handle dating an older woman? This went way past cougar, despite her looking no more than thirty.

For a moment he didn't say anything. Then he chuckled. "Doggone, you look good for a ninety-three-year-old."

She grinned. "Thanks. You're not upset?"

"Why would I be?"

"Well, there's a bit of an age difference."

He was quiet a moment. She thought he was about to say something, then he shook his head. "Age is just a number, right?"

"Right." She felt a rush of relief he wasn't running the other direction.

"What happened to the asylum?"

She blinked at the swift change of subject. "What do you mean?"

He slanted her a knowing look.

She grinned. "Let's just say by the time I was done with it, there wasn't a brick standing."

As they pulled up in front of her house, she realized for the first time in a long time she felt hopeful. Not about life—life was always hopeful. But about love. It had been a very long time since anyone had made her feel that a relationship was possible.

Noah let out a huge sigh. "I shouldn't do this."

"Shouldn't do what?"

He leaned over and kissed her. His lips were soft, warm from the sun, and spicy from the noodles. His tongue, as it slipped into her mouth to toy with hers, was velvety. Erotic. She wrapped her arms around his neck, and he tugged her tight against him.

Oh, goddess, the man knew how to kiss. And how ridiculous. She saw....

Freaking fireworks. Really? Can you get any more cliché? And oh my goddess, is that a freaking violin?

Potions, Poisons and Peril

CHAPTER

THIRTEEN

If Lene and Veri were surprised when Noah showed up, they kept it to themselves. Mostly. Veri slid Emory a sidelong look that spoke volumes. Lene snickered and asked him if he was in the mood for something sweet before shoving a plate of macadamia nut cookies in his face.

Edwina was the last to arrive. She wore flowing robes of midnight-blue silk that made her gray eyes pop. Her dark hair—liberally streaked with gray—was done up in a messy bun and secured with silver hairpins, which had dangling charms shaped like moons and stars. She wore a massive silver ankh around her neck, the center of which was a turquoise-blue scarab. As usual, her face was makeup free, and her feet were in Doc Martens.

"I know, I know. I look ridiculous," she said, sweeping into the living room. "But it's for the customers. Just got done with a séance. People expect a certain…" She twirled her hand in the air as if fishing for a word. "A certain stylistic appearance from their mediums."

"Naturally," Emory said, repressing a grin. Edwina's eschewing of proper atmosphere didn't extend to her person "Come in and make yourself comfortable."

Edwina dropped down dead center on the cream-colored couch, propping her boots on the scarred coffee table Emory had inherited from her aunt. "Very comfy." She looked approvingly at the three-foot-tall amethyst geode in one corner and the salt tea lights on the mantel.

Emory had pulled the blue and cream toile drapes closed over the windows so as not to give the neighbors an eyeful. But she'd hated closing out the scent of roses, so she cut a couple dozen and spread them around the room in crystal vases.

Lene offered her the plate of cookies, and Edwina helped herself to three. She tucked two into her pockets and quickly ate the third. She clapped her hands. "Shall we get started? Let's all take hands. You, too, Noah. You sit beside me." She patted the empty spot on her left.

He joined her, playing the good sport. Veri took the spot on Edwina's other side. Once they were all in a circle, Edwina had them reach across arms of furniture to take each other's hands.

"Helps with the energy flow," she assured them. Once everyone was in position to her satisfaction, she ordered them to focus on the dead men. She closed her eyes, inhaled, and blew out a deep breath. Several breaths later she opened her eyes and shook her head. "This is ridiculous. They're being most unhelpful."

"Who?" Veri asked suspiciously.

"My contacts, of course. Who do you think?" Edwina rolled her broad shoulders. "Let me try again. *Focus* people."

They focused.

A few minutes later Edwina let out a deep sigh. "This is what I got. These men had something the killer wanted."

Veri huffed dramatically. "As if we hadn't figured that out."

Edwina ignored her. "It doesn't feel like the deaths were planned. They were more a side effect. Unintended."

They'd figured that out, too. "Anything else?" Emory asked.

"Afraid that's it. They're being irritatingly silent on the subject. I'm sorry. It was worth a try."

"Thanks anyway."

"Wait!" Edwina held up a finger. "Tea."

They exchanged glances. "What?"

"This has something to do with tea."

"Um, can you give us anything more?" Emory asked. "Like what tea? How is it involved?"

"Sorry, no." Edwina stood and swiped another couple of cookies from the plate. "But if I can help you with anything else, let me know. My door is always open." She paused. "Try not to find any more dead bodies. I dislike the swamp." She bid them goodbye and hustled out the door. On the doorstep, she turned back. "One more thing. The young witch."

Emory said, "Mia?"

"That's the one. You must guide her, Emory. You must. For if she is lost, evil will have gained a powerful ally." With that she was gone, leaving Emory staring after her.

"That was weird," Lene said, peering over Emory's shoulder.

Veri snorted. "Bet she's a fake."

"You think everyone's a fake," Lene said. "You know very well she practices."

"I assure you, Edwina is not a fake," Noah said. "But like most psychics, the information she receives isn't always clear."

"I didn't know she was supposed to be psychic," Veri said tartly.

"She's a lot of things," Emory said.

Veri huffed. "If you say so. Anyway, I gotta move. Hot date." She gave Noah a peck on the cheek, waved airily to the rest of them, and followed Edwina out the door.

"Guess that's my cue to leave," Lene said with a smirk. "See you tomorrow." She shot Emory another smirk before departing.

She wasn't sure what to do. Should she offer him tea? A beer? Something stronger? Offer to show him her butterfly collection? Not that she had one. She opened her mouth to say something, she wasn't sure what.

He spoke first. "I've got to go, too. I'm seeing Mitch's mother tomorrow. Tell her what happened."

"Is that wise? I mean, we buried him. There's no police report or anything. What if she starts asking questions?"

"She won't. She's his only living relative and has late-stage Alzheimer's. She won't remember, but she still has a right to know. Mitch was awarded a Purple Heart. She should have that."

Emory nodded. "I get that. I am really sorry about his death. I know he was your friend. I wish we could have stopped this all before…."

"Hey, it's not your fault. It's the fault of whoever is doing this."

She still felt guilty. If only she could have figured out the spell faster. But then that hadn't told her much anyway.

"I'll see you tomorrow," he said softly. He leaned down and pressed his lips to hers.

Caught by surprise, she gasped. His tongue slid past her lips, teasing, tasting. Her gasp turned to a sigh as he pulled her closer. She could feel every inch of him, hard against her softness. Heat enveloped her as he took the kiss deeper, turning her brain to mush. There went those freaking violins again.

Then he was gone, melting into the night as if he'd never been there.

CHAPTER
FOURTEEN

Lene strode into the shop, the bell above the door tinkling merrily. "Last night was interesting." She had on knee-length red pants and a white T-shirt stamped with an image of General Organa, with the words "A woman's place is in the Resistance." Her blonde hair was piled on top her head, and her lips matched her pants. She was holding a hot pink box, which she set down on the counter. She flipped open the lid and selected a raspberry-filled donut.

"You're telling me. I was hoping Edwina could tap into something more. I'm not sure what we got is going to be terribly helpful," Emory said, grabbing a maple bar. Sugary sweetness exploded on her tongue. She looked over the order form she was filling out, double checking she'd got everything. "I need to get in touch with Mia again, too. You heard what Edy said about her."

"I did, but that is not what I meant," Lene said, giving her a sly look as she took a giant bite of her donut.

"What do you mean?" She played innocent.

Lene leaned across the counter, flashing a large portion of her ample bosom. "Rumor has it you had a hot date with the mysterious Noah Laveau. Spill it, girl. I want to hear everything!"

She shushed her as the two customers in the shop glanced up, startled and clearly curious by her outburst

Emory gave them a smile. "Hi, ladies. Welcome to Healing Herbs. Let me know if you need anything."

They went back to browsing the scented candle selection, but there was no doubt they were still listening.

"Come on, what happened? Give me all the juicy details," Lene whispered, practically dancing with excitement.

"Don't you have a store to run?"

Lene waved her off. "I'll open when I open. Spill."

Emory shrugged as if it were no big deal, but it was a big deal. A very big deal, and Lene knew it. It had been years since Emory had been in an intimate relationship with a man, not that she and Noah had gotten that far yet. Decades since she'd let her guard down enough to let anyone get close to her, never mind a date.

"How was he? I bet he was amazing. All that experience."

"I didn't sleep with him, Lene. It's too early for that."

Lene snorted. "Are you kidding me? No such thing as too early in my book. You gotta try out the merchandise, am I right? Seriously, girl, you need to get laid before your lady parts shrivel up and die."

Emory's cheeks pinkened. "Oh, hush. Go read a book or something, will you? I'm busy."

Lene laughed and sauntered out the door. "Fine. Time to open the bookstore anyway. But I'll be back."

Emory ignored her and refocused on the order, but her mind was elsewhere. Lene was exaggerating about her lady parts, surely. But she wasn't ready to sleep with Noah. Not just yet. Because he was more than fling material. Frankly, he was amazing, and that scared her to death.

Her mother had fallen in love with a man, let down her guard, and invited him into her life. She'd told him the truth about herself, showed him what she could do. And for that she'd spent the rest of her life locked up in the looney bin, sedated to the point of being catatonic. Emory had very nearly gone the same way. That's what happened when you put your trust in a man.

Granted Noah was aware of things supernatural. He had Veri for a cousin, and he already knew what Emory was. He likely wasn't going to lock her away or put her on medication. But the idea of opening herself up completely to him, of being totally honest and vulnerable, was absolutely terrifying.

The bell jingled again. Susan hovered just inside the entrance. She was wearing a big, floppy straw hat and mirrored sunglasses, as if trying to go incognito, but she blended in about as well as a poppy among daisies.

Emory waved her over. She fast-walked to the counter, head down, as if that way no one would notice her. "You're early. You were supposed to come by tomorrow."

"I'm on my lunch," she whispered, shooting Emory a look above her sunglasses. "But I need to know what you found. I couldn't wait for tomorrow."

"He's not under a spell, Susan," she whispered back. "There is nothing magical going on."

"Something has to be wrong. It was such a sudden change. He's never been this way before."

Emory had her doubts, but she murmured in sympathy. "I don't know why he changed suddenly. Could be something biological. Could be stress at work. I don't know. But something is going on. He's an abuser. He's abusing you. You need to leave him."

Susan shook her head emphatically. "No. I don't believe in divorce."

"Then don't divorce him. Just leave. It's the only way you'll be safe." Emory handed her a pamphlet. "Here's information on what to do. Places to go for help. These people can help you."

"Can't you put a spell on him to make him stop? Deep down he's a good man."

"I'm sorry, I can't do that. I can't interfere with a person's free will. He won't change, Susan. I promise you that. Abusers don't. They promise all sorts of things, but they never change."

Susan stiffened her spine. "Then I will pray for him, but I'm not leaving. Fat lot of help you are." And with that she marched out, leaving the pamphlet on the counter.

"Maybe she'll change her mind," Lene said softly. Emory hadn't heard her walk up.

"Maybe, but she's the only one who can make that decision." Emory only hoped she did so before it was too late.

The rest of the week passed painfully slowly. Edwina checked in a couple times to see how the investigation was going. The answer was pretty much nowhere. The news was still reporting random people going crazy. Susan didn't return, which was expected, but neither did Mia, which had Emory worried. She hadn't answered phone calls or texts.

Edy's words echoed in Emory's mind. The need to help the young witch grew with every passing moment.

Noah stopped by the shop nearly every day with lunch or coffee, and they'd talk about mundane, stupid things. It didn't matter what they discussed. She was just happy to be near him.

"Why don't we go out tonight?" he suggested.

"I'd love to go dancing."

"That would be enjoyable."

She was surprised. "No protestations about how you can't dance or hate dancing or how real men don't dance?"

"I realize this current trend for macho nonsense among the male population disallows the pleasure of dancing, but once upon a time, it was the mark of a real man to master the intricate dances of the court. A man who refused to dance with his woman was considered a coward."

"Huh. Sounds like a very enlightened time. I didn't realize you were a history geek."

He gave her a grin. "I like old things."

That was the thing about witches in general and portal witches in particular. The practice of magic could sap the life and vitality out of you, but it also had a way of replenishing you. Especially the power of the portals. While they could kill her if she wasn't careful, she also drew energy from them, as had her mother before her, and her grandmother before that, and so on to the beginning of the portalways.

Technically a portal witch could live indefinitely, although the oldest she'd heard of was 500. Most didn't make it past two centuries. They got arrogant, sloppy, and eventually were overloaded. Or they got killed by their neighbors, like her mother. The Witch Trials had been long over when her mother died, locked up in that horrible place, but they'd killed her just the same.

"Any recommendations?" he asked.

"I know a good salsa place if you like Latin dancing."

"Perfect."

"It gets a little wild, though," she warned him.

His smile turned wolfish. "Even better."

The minute Emory stepped through the door, the cheerful Latin beat put a smile on her face. She moved to the rhythm in a subtle shift of hips and feet. Noah kept one arm firmly around her, and she swayed closer, already half-drunk with the feel of him and intoxicated by the sensual beat of the music.

He scanned the crowd, seemingly unaffected by the sexily dressed female dancers flashing cleavage and thigh as they shimmied against their male partners. The salsa club was on the other side of town from her house, but it was worth the drive. She enjoyed the fun atmosphere and the chance to get out and move. And she never lacked for a dance partner. Sometimes Lene and Veri came with her. Other times she met up with mundane acquaintances. Sometimes it was nice to just get away from the whole witch thing for a while and be normal.

A woman in a short red dress and strappy black sandals with heels about three feet tall waved. She smiled and waved back.

"Friend of yours?" he asked.

"Sort of. I met her here. She's a mundane."

The woman eyeballed Noah and shot a thumbs-up. Emory laughed.

He dragged her to the middle of the dance floor, calmly nudging everyone out of the way. Nobody argued, they just moved. He stopped under the swirling disco ball and yanked her up against him so she could feel his heat through her clothes. She blushed.

Whatever he may have learned in the military, he seemed to have his dance moves down pretty well. He danced with fluid grace, hands gliding over her body. She had the feeling this was it. Tonight he was definitely coming home with her.

And then someone screamed. High-pitched, female, infused with pure horror. Another woman joined in, then another. The crowd parted like the Red Sea. Noah froze, shoving her behind him protectively. She tried to get around him, but his grip was firm on her arm, so she stopped struggling and peered around him. In the middle of the dance floor was a body. A very dead body. Even from a distance, she saw sigils dancing in the air above it.

CHAPTER
FIFTEEN

Noah grabbed Emory before she could run to the body. "Let me go," she hissed, annoyed at his manhandling.

"Wait Do you really want to expose your abilities in front of this crowd?"

He had a point. The last thing she needed was an entire club full of mundane humans having a meltdown over witches and magic.

"What do we do?" she whispered.

"We let the cops handle it, of course. That's their job." He started for the door.

She tugged at his arm. "Wait, Noah. The guy was killed by the same spell used on the others."

He stopped and turned to her. "Are you sure?"

"Positive."

"There's no way we can prevent the police from looking into this."

Which could lead them to Gary and Mitch. "I know, but I need to study the body before the cops come if we're to learn anything."

His jaw flexed. "Do you have any idea how dangerous this is?"

"I do, but this is part of what I do. It's who I am. I have to walk the spell before it fades."

"Let me at least get the crowd under control before you start. Minimize the exposure."

He was right. They had to keep this under the radar, or they might start a panic. Living in a town of witches was one thing. Knowing magic was killing people was another.

"Do it, but make it fast. The spell is already fading."

He nodded and disappeared. A moment later he reappeared with an enormous man who had "bouncer" practically engraved on his forehead. The sleeves of his black tee were stretched to the limit, revealing massive biceps and forearms with a light dusting of dark hair. He was handsome in a rugged way but scary as heck.

"All right, people, move back and give the man some air," the bouncer boomed. He waved them back, huge shoulder muscles flexing under the thin material of his shirt.

The crowd moved back eagerly, which was ridiculous. The man did not need air. The man was dead.

A woman piped up, "I'll call an ambulance." She rummaged in her bag.

"Make it quick," Noah murmured. "The authorities will be here soon, and we need to be gone by then."

"I have to get closer. Won't the bouncer wonder...?"

"I told him you're a doctor."

"Okay." She hoped no one asked her why it hurt when they coughed, or she was going to be royally screwed.

She went over to the corpse and pretended to take his pulse. Her brain went fuzzy, and her hands started to shake.

Was the heart on the right or the left? She wasn't used to working in front of a crowd.

Unlike the last two victims, this man was young. No more than twenty-five. His pale blond hair was plastered to his face by sweat, either from dancing or a reaction to the spell. His hazel eyes stared blankly at her, devoid of the life. She tried to ignore the death stare, although it gave her the creeps, and concentrated on the images dancing above him.

She mentally traced each symbol, taking in every detail, from the tiniest curlicue to the faintest color shift. What she really needed was paper. She needed to record these images while they were fresh. She might discover more about the spell. Even trace it back to the caster. There was no way she could do that in front of all these people, so she focused on committing each one to memory.

Emory looked up. "We should check his ID, don't you think?" She really preferred not to dig through a dead man's pockets if she didn't have to, especially with everyone watching.

Noah muttered something to the bartender, who strode to one of the round tables dotting the edge of the dance floor and whipped off the tablecloth, scattering half empty glasses and used napkins. He handed it to Noah and returned to glaring at the customers.

Noah spread the tablecloth over the man like a blanket. "I told him the guy was in shock and needed to be kept warm," he whispered.

"Good thinking."

While pretending to tuck the blanket around the victim, he pulled a smartphone and a black nylon wallet out of the man's pockets. The wallet was the cheap kind, with a Velcro closing and a washed-out image of a comic book character on the front. He rummaged through it, pulling out a driver's license.

"Zach Polinsky. He was only twenty-three. Poor kid." Using his body to hide his actions he handed Emory the license. "Nothing useful on his phone."

It had either been unlocked or one of Noah's many skills was hacking smartphones. "What about car keys?" She studied Zach's license. He lived on the outskirts of Deepwood in the more run-down part of town. She handed the license back.

He took a snapshot of the license and put it back in the wallet, tucking it and the phone back in the victim's pockets. "Got them." He dangled the keys in front of her.

In the distance a siren wailed. The crowd stirred restlessly and then, almost as one, charged for the door. The bouncer didn't even try to stop them.

"We've got to go now." He dragged her to her feet, and she followed him to the exit.

"Hey, wait!" the bouncer shouted. "You need to stay and talk to the cops." But they were already out the door and halfway across the parking lot.

"What about the cops?" she asked. "They're going to know we were here. What if they find us? We could get arrested."

"Don't worry. I'll take care of it."

"How? Are you magically going to erase our images from everyone's cell phones? And what about fingerprints?"

He gave her a look she couldn't interpret. She suddenly wondered exactly what he'd done for the army.

"This is the third body in, what, a week-and-a-half? This is not boding well." She really needed an aspirin. Or a large glass of vodka.

"We haven't had a lot of leads." There was no censure in his voice, but she still felt guilty. She was the one who hadn't been able to figure out what the spell did or where it came from.

He hit the button on Zach Polinsky's car fob. A vehicle halfway down the street flashed its lights. "There."

"Let's check out his car and apartment. Maybe we'll luck out."

Zach Polinsky drove a junky import that had seen better days, those days being somewhere around 1989. It was midnight blue except for one door, which was burnt orange. A giant rust spot decorated the hood, the wire antennae was bent almost in half and sported a shredded flag of indeterminate nature.

"Let's hurry," Emory urged. Without the keys, and with a dead body to deal with, the police wouldn't find the car right away. They had time, but they needed to make it fast.

He pulled a pair of rubber gloves out of his back pocket and snapped them on. They were thin and black, like the kind seen on crime shows.

"Seriously? You carry gloves around with you?"

He smirked. "Don't want to leave prints."

"We touched the license and wallet."

"Don't worry about it. It's covered." A quick rifling through the car yielded nothing but the fact that Zach Polinsky was inordinately fond of fast food and Jolly Rancher candies. The tassel from his high school graduation was still hanging from the cracked rearview mirror, its shiny threads faded by the sun. The car smelled like stale fries and mildew.

Noah tossed the keys inside, locked and shut the door, and stripped off his gloves. "No sign of the spell?"

"*Nada.*" She hadn't noticed any sign of it inside the club either, except on Zach. "He must have been dosed before he got here. At home, probably. Unless he stopped off somewhere first."

Always a possibility, of course, but she was betting his death somehow tied into all the others. "So we visit his apartment next. Maybe we'll get lucky."

Noah gave her a meaningful look. She ignored him. She did not need to be distracted in the middle of an investigation.

Investigation? Who was she, Jessica Fletcher? Her life had taken a decided turn for the interesting lately.

They got into Noah's jeep and drove to the apartment building where Zach had lived, fingers crossed he didn't have roommates or anything. It was one of those ugly, squatty things that had been built in the '70s. It looked like it hadn't been painted since then either, the peeling paint still vaguely mustard yellow and poop brown. The parking lot asphalt was chock-full of potholes, weeds springing up between the cracks. It was filled with ancient mini-vans and well-worn sedans whose dependability was doubtful at best. Half of them were missing hubcaps.

They trudged up the outside steps to the second floor and went along the walkway to number 23. Noah rapped on the door. No answer. He pulled out a set of picks and expertly popped the lock.

She shot him a look. "You just walk around carrying lock picks?"

"I have since I met you," he said wryly.

The inside of Zach's apartment was a lot like the inside of his car. It stank of stale food and something vaguely rotten. A pile of pizza boxes, with remnants of fossilized crusts, were stacked on the stained carpet next to the couch. Dirty dishes were piled high in the sink, and the garbage was overflowing with empty beer cans, some of which were scattered across the grimy linoleum floor. A mound of dirty clothes blocked half the hallway to the bedroom. There was no washer or dryer in the unit that Emory could see. A video game poster, hanging on the wall behind the couch, was the only decoration. The place was in dire need of a makeover. Or a can of gasoline and a match.

"See anything?" Noah asked.

She shook her head and edged into the kitchen. Keeping her hand covered with a tissue, she opened the cupboard doors. Most of them were empty, but in one she found a half empty box of saltines, a large container of table salt, and a red tea tin. The moment she took the lid off, symbols exploded into the air. Inside were nestled half a dozen tea bags.

"I think we have a winner."

Potions, Poisons and Peril

CHAPTER
SIXTEEN

Back in the car, Emory clutched the tea tin in her lap, feeling the warmth of the spell radiating inside. It was strong, whatever it was. Stable, too. Not fading at all, unlike what it did when it hit its victims' systems. She inspected the tin in the dim light from the streetlamps.

"There's a label." She switched on the map light and squinted at the worn lettering. "Té. I know this place. It's a few blocks from my shop."

"Seems like we should be asking questions there, then."

"They're closed tonight, but we can hit them first thing in the morning. And we should check with Edwina. She knows just about everything there is to know about the shops on our street." She bit her lip. "Now what?"

"Now dinner."

She slid him a sidelong look. "I could eat."

"Good. There's this place I heard about. Really... unique."

She grew instantly suspicious. "How unique?"

He flashed a heart-melting grin. "You'll see."

The restaurant was about ten miles out of town on a nearly disused highway. Like every other diner everywhere it had a simple brick exterior with lots of windows. The interior was cheap tile and vinyl booths in dire need of a makeover. The pies in the glass case up front looked delicious, though.

"This is 'special?'" she couldn't help asking. What was with him taking her to "special" places?

His eyes sparkled with amusement. "Just wait."

The waitress, dressed in a cheap, polyester uniform of blue and brown, picked up a couple of laminated menus. "Two?"

"I'd like to speak to Mr. Smith."

Laying the menus down next to the register, she nodded briefly, her brown ponytail bobbing. Her eyelids fluttered, revealing eyeshadow that matched her uniform. "No problem. I'll get him."

She disappeared through the door leading to the kitchen. A couple minutes passed before a man appeared through the same door. He was nearly as short as Emory and almost as round as he was tall, with about six strands of hair on top his nearly bald head. Beads of sweat dotted his pale forehead, which he blotted with a red handkerchief. His cheeks were flushed pink, as though he was overwarm and the armpits of his white shirt were ringed with sweat. He adjusted his brown-and-blue striped tie and peered first at Noah and then Emory. She wasn't picking up anything supernatural about him, but that didn't necessarily mean anything. Some supernaturals had the ability to mask their true selves, even from witches.

"How may I help you?" His voice was surprisingly high-pitched.

"A good friend of mine, Miss Edwina Gale, recommended your establishment," he said.

Vale's eyes widened. "Ms. Gale? Indeed. Please follow me."

"No way Edwina recommended this restaurant," she murmured. Edwina enjoyed a good diner as much as anyone—she owned one—but this did not look like a good diner.

He smiled. "I assure you, she did."

"I don't see her in a place like this. Are you sure?"

"Certain."

"What is this place exactly?"

"Like I said, you'll see."

They followed Mr. Smith down a short hallway to the bathrooms. He pulled out a key, unlocked the door marked Employees Only, and waved them inside. It was a one-holer; sink, toilet, and a rack of cleaning supplies. Smith strode to the rack and fiddled with something on one of the shelves. The shelf swung away from the wall, revealing a door. This was like something out of a Bond movie.

"Where the Hades are you taking me?" Emory asked.

"I promise it will be worth it. That, or I'm killing Edwina later."

Emory, amused by the cloak-and-dagger feel of things, followed Mr. Smith into a small antechamber that had been painted rich blood red and carpeted in thick, charcoal-colored carpet. A chandelier dripping with clear black crystals hung overhead, its light casting rainbows across the room. Directly opposite them was another door, painted black. There was no doorknob. Mr. Smith closed the bathroom door behind them, and the room began to move.

She clutched Noah's arm. "What the...?"

145

"Elevator. We're going down."

The elevator halted, and the door slid open silently. Smith waved them out but remained inside, clearly not planning to follow them. "Enjoy."

Noah gave him one of his regal nods and held the door for her. She stepped into wonderland.

Above them was a sky full of stars, twinkling against the unending blackness of space. There were constellations she'd never seen in patterns that were totally unfamiliar. She could barely pull her gaze away.

The floor was an ocean of blue marble streaked with veins of green and white in a breathtaking pattern. They met in the middle of the room, shooting up to the sky and out in a spray of sea foam carved so delicately, she wondered why it didn't shatter. The sculpture glowed as if lit from within, the translucent marble turning to greenish-blue luminescence, like a sea creature from the deepest depths.

Scattered across the marble ocean were dozens of delicate round tables with fluted legs that looked as if they'd been carved from ice. On each table a white candle burned, adding its warm glow to the magic. Around the tables were couples and small groups, chattering in a multitude of languages. Hidden from view live music played, but it was like nothing she'd heard before. It was haunting. Alien.

She realized she was clutching Noah's arm. "What is this place?"

He laid his hand over hers. She shivered at his touch. "Welcome," he said, "to Fairy."

CHAPTER
SEVENTEEN

"Say what?" Emory stared, suddenly realizing few of the patrons were human.

Although some looked human—she was guessing they were witches, like her, or possibly fairy folk—others looked alien. The blue cast to their skin wasn't from the sculpture, as she'd first thought. They were actually blue. And green. And... "Is that woman purple?"

"Don't stare. It's rude."

"I'm sorry, I just... Fairy?" *And purple freaking aliens? How did aliens get to Fairy?*

"It's just a small portion, of course. Almost like an outpost. Open to anyone who knows how to get here."

"That's fascinating."

A gentleman strode toward them, dressed in flowing silk robes of white and blue. Judging by his tall stature and delicate features, he was clearly fae. He bowed deeply. "My lord. My lady. Allow me to show you to your table." He whirled in a swirl of silk and strode back the way he'd come, with Emory and Noah close on his heels. He seated them at one of the impossibly delicate tables before bowing again and disappearing.

"This is a fairy restaurant?"

Noah grinned, a flash of brightness that sent her pulse into overdrive. "Everything on the menu is from recipes of the Otherworld. The fairy realm. Some are over 10,000 years old."

"Holy goddess." She rapped on the table, trying to figure out what it was made of.

"Crystalline marble," he said. "Not native to Earth."

"I think you'd better explain." There were a lot of things in this world that were hidden from human view, but as a witch, she was privy to most of them. This was totally new to her. "How the Hades does Edwina know about this place, and why did she tell you?" Why not tell the coven?

He was silent as a woman in black silk robes glided up to the table and poured a dark wine into their glasses, then glided away. Emory eyed her glass suspiciously. It looked like normal red wine, only a little darker. She took a tentative sip. Tasted like normal wine, too. Really, really good wine.

"You know Edwina is a witch."

"Uh-huh," Emory said. "But so am I, and I've never heard of this place."

"Edwina knows a lot of things ordinary people don't."

"You're telling me, but that doesn't explain *how* she knows about it."

"She told me she dated a fae once."

She blinked, unsure what to think of that. She, too, had dated a fae, but he'd been a jerk, and he'd definitely not brought her here. "But why would she tell *you?*"

"The Laveaus are an old, trusted family among the supernatural sets," he reminded her. "We have proven ourselves trustworthy and hold many secrets."

"True. So, this place? How did it get into the basement of a diner in the middle of nowhere?"

"It's not exactly in the basement of a diner. Those are real stars." He glanced up, and her gazed followed.

She stared at what she'd assumed was a painted ceiling. "Sweet goddess above. We passed through the Veil, didn't we?"

"We did."

The Veil was hard to explain. Best way she could describe it was that it was like a curtain between layers, or dimensions, of the universe. Normally the Veil was solid, like a wall. But sometimes it thinned to almost nothing, allowing a person to pass to the other side.

"Somebody decided to open a restaurant in Fairy?" She was surprised there was no mention of it in the grimoires of the portal witches. Then again, portals were a different thing from the Veil. Sort of connected but not exactly.

"This restaurant was created in a pocket of Fairy, partitioned off from the rest of the realm. It was designed after the Royal Court of Atlantis. The ballroom, actually. It was considered one of the most beautiful places in Atlantis. A group of artisans worked together for months to recreate it."

"You sure know a lot about this place." She eyed him suspiciously. What wasn't he telling her?

"Like I said, my family is privy to many secrets."

She was going to have to ask Veri about that. She would have asked more questions, but the black-robed woman reappeared with an elaborately filigreed serving tray containing two gold and crystal wine goblets and a matching pitcher and bowl. She lowered the tray to the table, picked up a pair of gold tongs, and fished a large, blue ball from the bowl. She dropped it into one of the glasses. She dropped a second blue ball into the other glass. Picking up the pitcher, she poured pale yellow liquid into each glass before placing it in front of Emory. Once Noah had his glass, the woman retreated with the tray.

"What's this?" Veri asked.

"A cocktail. Watch." Noah's eyes were on his own glass.

Slowly, the blue ball changed to dark purple. Then violet. And finally, magenta.

"What is it?" she asked, astonished.

"The ball is made from the tea of a very special flower. When liquor is added, it changes color. Smell it."

Emory gave a cautious sniff. "Yum. It smells like Fruit Loops."

He chuckled. "Taste."

She took a sip and flavor exploded across her tongue. "It's like a grown-up Sweet Tart. I could drink these all day!"

"Just don't drink them too fast. They're potent."

Once again, the woman arrived at their table carrying a large, gold platter. She set it down gently and retreated.

The platter was piled high with what looked like gelatin cubes in various colors. Each one was about an inch square.

The smile on Noah's face as he gazed at it was so wide, it was blinding. Like a kid at Christmas who'd just gotten everything on his letter to Santa.

"You've eaten this stuff before?" she asked.

"Once or twice. Dig in," he said, grabbing a cube of whatever it was.

She assumed it was food since Noah was munching away, beaming at her. There were no utensils of any kind, so she selected a red cube—she usually liked red candy—and ate it, chewing cautiously. She'd expected something fruity, but that was definitely not what she got. The taste could only be described as umami, like beef with vegetables in a rich, herbal sauce. The texture was closer to that of a jelly bean than Jell-O. It was the most bizarre combination of flavor and texture she'd ever experienced.

"That was... unexpected."

Noah beamed. "Try another."

This time she selected a yellow cube. "Tastes like chicken."

"Close enough. The actual animal is extinct on Earth now, but it was very much like chicken, or so I've heard."

"This is what fairies eat?" The ones who lived on Earth ate human food.

"Of course. Very efficient. Delicious, and all the nutrients required without the extras you don't need. They eat other things, too." He motioned to a table nearby, where the inhabitants were eating noodles similar to what Aulii had served them. "But this is some of the best."

"I see." Not Emory's idea of a gourmet meal, but when in Rome. Or Fairy, rather. She tried a blue cube and made a face. It tasted like beets. She loathed beets. It was like eating dirt.

"You don't like it, do you?"

"It's different. I'm having a hard time wrapping my head around this as food. I feel like it should be sweet. You know, candy."

He grinned. "Then you're going to enjoy this." He waved at someone across the room, and the server reappeared, whipping the tray of cubes away and replacing it with a different tray of cubes. Instead of jewel tones, the cubes were pastel colors: pink, peach, lemon yellow, white, pale blue.

151

Noah pushed the tray toward her with a smile. She hesitantly selected a peach-colored cube and bit into it. An explosion of flavor exploded across her tongue.

"Holy Hades, this tastes like chocolate. And raspberries? With cream! Oh, my goddess." She grabbed another peach cube and chewed, moaning.

"Try a white one," he said, handing her one of the semi-translucent squares.

A burst of something citrusy and sweet filled her mouth, and she moaned again. Noah's eyes darkened as he licked his full lips. "Lemon merengue," she whispered.

"Close enough." His voice was hoarse. The look he gave her could have melted an iceberg, and she wasn't even close to cold.

She cleared her throat. "I think I'm still hungry." She didn't mean food.

He frowned for a moment and then his face cleared. "I think I've got something that will fix that."

"Oh, good," she whispered, shivering with anticipation as he pulled her from the table.

Once outside, he pulled her into his arms and kissed her. It was deep and sweet and hot all at the same time.

He pulled away only to stare down at her. "Are you sure?"

"Yes."

CHAPTER
EIGHTEEN

As Emory stepped through the door to the tea shop, Té, warm, humid air hit her in the face. The shop was in an old, red caboose. A few years back, it had been part of an antique shop which encompassed the building next door, but it had gone out of business, and the buildings had been divvied up. The half on the left was now a bakery; the half on the right, including the caboose, was a tea shop.

The entrance was through the caboose. A flight of wooden stairs led down into the main part of the tearoom, where small, cozy tables and booths took up a narrow space. Hipsters with expensive computer gadgets and chunky framed glasses hunched over tables, oblivious to the world around them, steaming cups of tea lattes clutched in their beringed hands.

Emory remembered the many happy hours spent poking through antiques and imported goods in the large, windowed room when she was visiting her aunt. Now it was crammed with more tables and more hipsters. The bar was in the right-hand corner as one came down the stairs and had been designed to look like an old time apothecary shop, only this place dispensed tisanes, tea lattes, and scones instead of laudanum and Mrs. Murphy's Miracle Syrup.

"This is interesting," Noah said behind her. The way he said "interesting" did not indicate anything positive.

After a memorable and sleepless night, one that she'd never forget, they'd agreed to visit the tea shop together. Perhaps there they could find a lead to the killer.

One of the baristas—did they call them baristas in a tea shop? —a young man with enormous muttonchops and thick-lensed glasses, eyeballed them suspiciously. "What'll it be?" he asked in a snooty tone that made her want to reach over and shake him by his nose hairs. "You can get coffee next door at the bakery."

Curious that he automatically pegged her as a coffee drinker. She much preferred tea and blended her own, imbued with spellwork.

She set the tin they'd found at Zach's house on the counter. "I believe this came from your shop."

"So?"

"So, the tea is unique. I wondered what kind it was, as I'd like to purchase some."

He picked up the tin, turned it over, and set it back down with a shrug. "It's vintage Pu-Erh. Special order only and very expensive."

"So you don't carry it here in the shop?"

"No. Too pricey for the usual customer, but I can order some in if you like."

"Actually," she said, leaning on the counter, "what I really want is a list of customers who have bought this tea recently. Say, in the last month or two."

His eyes narrowed. "That's privileged information. I can't give that out." His tone said he wouldn't give it out regardless.

Some witches had the power to influence people with the tone of their voice or the power of their mind. Emory had no such abilities. Her only influence was a winning personality and ample cleavage, and so far, he'd been affected by neither. Time to send in the big guns. She stepped back and let Noah take over.

"Listen, buddy," Noah said, "this is really important. It may help us solve a murder."

The hipster dude snorted. When neither Noah nor Emory balked, the barista's eyes widened. "Seriously?"

They nodded.

"Are you cops?"

"Private investigators," she offered. It was sort of true. They were, investigating the deaths, even if nobody was footing the bill.

The barista snorted again. "Sorry. Still can't tell you." He started to turn away, but Noah grabbed his arm so fast, Emory gasped. The barista tried to shake him off. "Listen, mister, unless you're the police with a warrant, I'm not giving you a thing."

"Oh yes, you are, or I will ensure that you never enjoy the pleasures of the flesh again." His voice was a low, menacing growl that made the hairs on her arms stand up.

The barista blinked. "Are you threatening me, man?"

"I never threaten." His voice was cold. "I promise."

The scrawny guy swallowed, his Adam's apple bobbing in his skinny throat. "Whatever, man. I don't care. Let go of me, and I'll get you the info."

"Don't think I won't chase you down if you try to escape," Noah said.

He got a little paler, if that was possible. Noah released him and muttonchop boy quickly typed something into the computer. "In the last six months only three customers have ordered this particular tea." He hit a button, and Emory heard a printer below the counter spitting out ink. He reached down, grabbed the paper, and practically threw it at them. "There you go. Now get out of here before you get me into trouble."

"Thanks for your cooperation," she said sweetly. The barista snarled and gave her the finger. Noah grabbed her hand, and they hurried up the stairs and out onto the sidewalk. "I can't believe he actually gave the list to us," she said. "Way to shake him down."

"It's what I do."

She laughed. "Yes, you play the intimidation card rather well." She scanned the sheet of paper. "None of the victim's names are on here," she said. "So someone must have given it to them."

"Anyone stand out? Maybe someone with the title 'Evil Overlord' after their name?"

"No." She laughed. "That would be too easy. Let's go to my shop so I can research these people, maybe find a connection between them and the victims."

"You go ahead. I have a few things to take care of."

"Sure. I'll see you later?"

He gave her an abrupt nod before disappearing down the street. She stared after him, baffled. Apparently she was on her own.

"What did that tankard ever do to you?"

Noah glanced up from the pint of beer he'd been glaring at. Edwina loomed over him, her impressive bosom barely restrained by a lace-up bodice in a purple color. Her hair was done up in Princess Leia buns. She looked like she belonged at a Renaissance Faire or ComicCon.

"Just thinking," he said, raising his beer. It was good stuff, as beer went. He was more of a wine guy, but the bar was fresh out of moonberry wine. Imagine that.

Edwina sat on the barstool next to him. The bartender didn't even ask, just brought her a pint identical to Noah's.

She took a deep swig. "It's not honey mead, but it'll do."

The two of them stared at the television for a long moment. A sports game was playing, the volume off. In the background the old-fashioned jukebox cranked out an old Bon Jovi song. He could never remember the name of it, but he liked the heavy beat.

"I'm guessing you didn't call me here to brood over our beer," she said, breaking the silence. She tapped a short, lime green nail on the bar.

"I'm old."

"Aren't we all? I turn sixty-five next month. Never thought I'd see the day."

"I mean really old. Possibly the oldest."

She gave him a measured look. "And?"

He rubbed the bridge of his nose. "I don't know what to do."

"About?"

"Emory. She's the problem."

"Ah." Her eyes took on a knowing look. "You haven't told her what you are, have you?"

"She wasn't part of the plan."

Edwina barked a laugh. "You gotta know that any time you make plans, the universe is gonna delight in messing with them."

"True." He took another swallow of beer. "Trouble is, I have no idea what to do about it. About her. I've never felt this way about anyone."

"Ever?"

"Nope."

"That sucks. That's a long time to not feel that. I personally have been madly in love with at least three people in my life. Two were at the same time. Have you told her how you feel?"

He shook his head.

"Idiot."

"I know. But how am I supposed to explain that I'm older than dirt? Literally."

She smirked. "I don't know, but you better figure it out, or she is gonna have your plums on a stick. Roast 'em over her little witchy fire."

He winced. "Thanks for the visual."

"Listen." She shoved her empty glass away. "This is how I see it. You got two choices. Either forget the witch and go on about your business, or man up and face the consequences. Easy."

"Sure, easy." Except it wasn't. If he stayed it meant risking his heart, the one thing that had never been in danger before. That was scarier than facing a hundred insurgents.

She stood. "Good luck to you. You're going to need it."

"Thanks for nothing," he said drily.

"Hey, if it was me, the choice would be easy. But then I'm the kind of woman who takes what I want and hang the consequences." She winked and strode out of the bar.

He went back to glaring at his beer. Hang the consequences. Yeah, he could do that.

CHAPTER
NINETEEN

"Oh, he's cute," Lene said, peering over Emory's shoulder at the image of a dark-haired man with sleepy, bedroom eyes. "Who is he?"

"Lucien Antonelli. One of the people who purchased a special tea from the tea shop."

She frowned. "What's important about that?"

"It's the same tea I found in our third victim's house. It's how the killer bespelled the victims. It's special order tea, and only three people have purchased it in the past six months. Lucien Antonelli is one of them. I'm trying to determine if he is any relation to our victims."

"You mean that hottie might be the killer?" She sounded disappointed.

"Maybe. So far I can't find a connection between him and any of the dead people."

"Well, that's a relief. I'd hate to think someone that good-looking was a serial killer."

Emory rolled her eyes. "You've heard of Dahmer, right? Ted Bundy? Serial killers, both considered quite handsome, at least by some." They were definitely not to her taste. She preferred her men less…murdery.

"Such a waste." Lene drifted off to poke around in the sale bin.

"Don't you have a store to run?" Emory asked. She felt like she'd been asking that a lot lately.

"The shop's always dead this early, so I decided to push my opening time back an hour. You got me for thirty more minutes."

"Wonderful," Emory said dryly.

The bell jangled, and Veri breezed in with a tray of coffees and a box of donuts. "Hey, gorgeous ladies. What's happening? Brought sustenance."

"Don't you have a shop to maintain?" Emory asked, grabbing a donut.

"It's totally dead today, so I left Noah in charge. Virgil is trying something new. Lavender and thyme donuts. Not sure how I feel about them."

Emory nearly choked on a bite of donut. "You left Noah alone in a lingerie shop?"

"Sure. Why not? Man needs to earn his keep. Besides, I figured he'd bring in the ladies."

Emory had no doubt that was true.

"What are you up to?" Veri peered over Emory's shoulder, just as Lene had done a moment before.

"She's looking for serial killers," Lene said, taking a cappuccino and a donut.

"And you think Lucien is a serial killer?" Veri asked.

Emory glanced up. "You know him?"

"He's witchblood. Recently moved from Phoenix. His mom and mine were in the same coven back in the '60s." Like Emory, Veri looked no older than late twenties. She was, in fact, much closer to fifty.

"Is he a natural?" Emory asked. A true male witch was rare. While plenty of witchblood males carried the genetics to have daughters who were natural witches, few of them inherited abilities themselves.

"Yep. That's why I talked him into moving here. I figured he would find Portland more comfortable."

"Why haven't you suggested him for the coven?"

Veri smiled. "He's not a portal witch. Besides, he's already found a coven he likes. They do a lot of naked moonlight dancing and stuff. He's kind of hippie that way."

Which would explain the exotic tea. "When did he move here?"

"Couple months ago. Why?"

"Still in our time frame, unfortunately. I can't rule him out. What does he do for a living?"

"He's a veterinarian."

"So he loves animals. Perfect," Lene cooed, fluttering her lashes as she munched on a pink donut.

That was another mark in his favor. She had found nothing to suggest he had a habit of poisoning people with tea. She moved on to the next name on the list.

"Hey, send me his deets, will you?" Lene asked.

"Why?"

"So I can Facebook-stalk him." Emory and Veri stared at her. "What?" Lene said. "I'm not going to do anything weird."

Veri laughed. "Girl, if you want an introduction so bad, all you gotta do is ask. I'm outta here. Better check and see if Noah's burned the place down yet."

"Thanks for the coffee and donuts," Emory said. Veri waved and sashayed out the door, bell jingling as she went. Emory turned back to her research.

"Another hottie?" Lene asked. She caught sight of the next person of interest. "Oh. Never mind."

The second name on the list was Daisy Hu. She looked to be about seventy. Emory doubted she was going around bespelling people, but due diligence was required. A surface search revealed nothing of interest.

Number three wasn't a person. It was a business called the Green Leaf Clinic—which sounded like a marijuana dispensary—with an address about half a mile from Healing Herbs. She'd never heard of it, so she did a quick search online. It was a natural health and alternative medicine clinic, which didn't rule out cannabis. She couldn't immediately see the connection between such a place and her victims and decided to do a tracking spell.

The shop was empty except for Lene, so she opened up a web browser and pulled up a map of the local area. Then she entered each address of the three people who'd ordered the tea. After markers showed up, she focused on each one, muttering an incantation under her breath.

She took out the crystal she always wore on a chain around her neck and held it close to the screen. "Which of these is connected to the spell on the tea?"

She moved the crystal, touching it to each marker on the map. First Lucien Antonelli, then Daisy Hu, and finally the clinic. The crystal lit up like a Christmas tree on Green Leaf Clinic.

"Bingo," she whispered.

Lene of the bionic hearing piped up, "What is it? Did you find something?"

She smiled. "I think I found the killer."

Emory wanted to call Noah right away, or better yet, run next door to Veri's shop. She could use some pretty new underwear. That always gave a girl a confidence boost. Before she could do either, the shop door slammed open, and Mia marched in, a scowl on her face.

"Mia!" She came around from behind the register. "I've been trying to get hold of you."

"I know," the teen snarled. "You've been driving me nuts."

Emory tried not to laugh. "Sorry?"

The girl crossed her arms and glowered at Lene. "Whatever, lady. I got bigger problems."

"Like?"

"Can you help me with this?" She lifted her shirt to reveal a section of stomach. A very hairy stomach.

Emory blinked. "Oh, dear."

"Exactly." Mia dropped her shirt and continued her scowling routine.

"What in Hades happened?" she asked, leading her to the alcove for more privacy.

Mia slouched in a chair. "There's this girl in my neighborhood, right? She's a totally mean girl. Really nasty, you know?"

"I'm familiar with the type." Although it had been a long time since she'd seen the inside of a schoolroom, mean girls were universal and timeless. She'd been forced to deal

163

with more than one of them over the years, some of them old enough to know better.

"I was sick and tired of her picking on me, so I did something about it. I'm a witch. I should be able to defend myself." Mia's demeanor was belligerent.

Emory saw where this was going. "You cast a spell."

"Duh." Mia rolled her eyes in the way only a teenager can. "Only it bounced back." She pointed at her hairy stomach. "As you can see."

"Did any of the spell stick to the target?"

Mia grinned maliciously. "Some."

The spell was simple enough to fix. She could see it dancing around Mia like clowns at a circus. But fixing it wouldn't teach the girl any lessons. It would only mean bigger trouble in the long run. There was still that issue of Mia's visions and possible portal connection.

"You're aware, of course, of the rule of three."

Mia gave an irritated sigh. "Whatever I put out bounces back on me times three," she recited in a sing-song voice, as if she'd heard it a thousand times.

"Guess you didn't consider that when you put the spell on your... whatever she is."

"Frenemy."

"Okay."

"And I did. I just didn't care." Mia crossed her arms, her lip puckering in a pout that made her look far younger than her eighteen years.

"So you were willing to pay the price until it turned out to be an extreme need for Nair."

Mia glowered. "Whatever. Can you fix it?"

Emory nodded.

Mia's eyes narrowed. "But?"

"I won't. This is something you're going to have to fix yourself."

"But I don't know how," Mia whined.

"Then I guess you'd better learn before that hair starts spreading somewhere people can see it."

Mia's eyes widened in horror, and she let out a string of words Emory was pretty sure her mother never taught her.

Emory calmly wrote something on one of her business cards. "This is a book on responsible magical practices. You can download it as an e-book for a couple bucks. Once you've figured it out, we can work on it together."

"You're giving me homework?" Mia screeched, cheeks reddening.

She leaned forward. "Listen to me, Mia, and listen good. You know the rules of magic and yet you made the decision to break them. No one but you. You pulled a prank, and you got caught. Suck it up. You want to undo this mess? Figure it out. Because next time you lose your temper, you might kill somebody, and how do you imagine that will affect you?"

The teen paled, but she was still defiant. Emory got it. She'd once been young and new to her power. She'd been angry and tried to pay back the people who'd hurt her and her mother. But she'd paid a hefty price for it and learned her lesson. Mia was going to have to learn, too, or the price she paid might be steep indeed.

Snatching the card from Emory's hand, the girl stomped off, slamming the door behind her. She didn't even so much as offer a "thank you" or "goodbye." Mia would be back, if for no other reason than to fix the hair problem.

That was when it suddenly occurred to Emory that the person who put the spell on Gary, Mitch, and Zach should be getting some blowback from it. Except they weren't, or they'd be dead. Unless...

"What if the spell wasn't meant to harm them physically," she mused aloud, pacing. The scent of cinnamon tickled her nose. "The deaths could be accidental. Some sort of unforeseen side effect."

Fred bounced out of his cage onto the counter and stared at her as if to say, "Or?"

"Or there could be some really dark stuff going on." She hoped it was the former because the later was a whole other world of messy.

CHAPTER
TWENTY

"You think you know how we can find the killer?" Noah asked when he met Emory outside the shop after work.

"I think so. One of the customers who bought the tea is e Green Leaf Clinic, not far from here. Look." She pulled up the clinic's website on her phone and showed him.

"It's a natural health clinic. Okay. But I still don't see the connection."

"There isn't one that's obvious, but I did some scrying, and that clinic consistently came up in connection with the tea."

"Do you think our victims were seeing someone at the clinic?"

"That's my guess. Maybe it was given to them as part of their treatment."

"There are two naturopaths and one energy healer at the clinic. Who do you want to hit first?"

"I have a feeling we won't get far taking the direct route," Emory said. "Regulations and all that. They probably won't even confirm the victims were their patients."

"The clinic is closed for the night. How about a little late-night breaking and entering?"

"Oh, you do know how to show a girl a good time." She laughed.

He gave her a sultry smile. "You have no idea. I can show you now if you like."

She placed a hand on his chest, loving the feel of solid muscle beneath the soft fabric of his T-shirt. "I don't think we have time for you to show me before we go committing felonies. After."

"It's a date."

Be still my heart.

She was getting a little too familiar with the criminal act of breaking and entering. Emory considered herself a law-abiding citizen, but these were extenuating circumstances. She doubted the police would feel the same. Best not to get caught.

Noah was stunningly good at unlocking the back door and disarming the alarm.

"Had some experience with this, have you?" she asked.

"I've picked up a few skills here and there."

"I bet."

The clinic was dark except for a faint blue glow from the reception desk down the hall; someone had left a computer monitor on. Between them and the front office stretched a dark hallway with closed doors on either side. The door closest to Emory on the right-hand side was unlocked. She opened it, but it was too dark to see anything, so she pulled out her phone and used the flashlight app. Janitorial closet.

The door on the left-hand side was marked Employees Only. The dim light from the nearest streetlight revealed it to be the break room, complete with cozy couches and an expensive expresso machine.

"There's probably a main file room," she said. "They'll have all their patient files there."

He nodded, moving farther down the hall. About halfway along was a door marked Private. "What do you want to bet this is it?"

A few seconds later, he had the door unlocked. He pushed it open.

"That was fast."

"Flimsy lock. A child could open that thing."

Rows of open shelving crammed with manila file folders crowded the small space. The files were in alphabetical order, the unit nearest the door reserved for current patients.

She skimmed the files, grabbing the first one with a name she recognized. "Gary Poe was a patient." She flipped the file open. It was thin, only a few pages. "Looks like he came in for a consult. The naturopath who saw him diagnosed stress, prescribed a homeopathic, and recommended acupuncture and massage therapy. Only the one visit, the same day he died."

"The timing is suspicious, but I don't see anything that might lead us to our killer."

She shoved the folder back on the shelf and grabbed Mitch's file. It was quite a bit thicker that Gary's. "Second victim was a regular. Visits to the naturopath, massages, acupuncture, at least half a dozen homeopathies."

"None of which we found in his house," he pointed out. "Looks like someone cleared out anything that might lead them here. Was he seeing the same doctor as Poe?"

She flipped through the documents. "Nope. The other one, plus assorted practitioners, none of whom Gary saw."

"Blast."

She felt the same way. Was this a dead end, too? She searched for the file of the final victim, Zach, and found it. "They were all patients here, and like Gary, Zach had only one consult and a follow-up. No overlap, though."

"Surely they must have crossed paths with someone here." He paced the small space, raking his hands through his short hair.

Emory thoughtfully tapped the file with a fingernail before sliding it back into place. "Who is the one person everyone entering this clinic would talk to before seeing anyone else?"

"Honestly? No clue. I don't spend a lot of time in doctors' offices."

She smiled. "I'll give you a hint." She beckoned him to follow her and slipped out the door into the hall. She nodded toward the glow at the front desk.

His expression cleared. "The receptionist."

"Exactly." She crossed her arms. "I think we need to stop by tomorrow and have a word with whoever sits behind that desk."

"Sounds like a plan." He pulled her into a hug. "How would you like to spend the time till then?"

She grinned. "I can think of a thing or two."

170

This was it. He had to tell her. He couldn't let this go any further without her knowing the truth. Should he tell her in the car or wait until they got inside? Inside. Yeah, he'd wait until they got to her place.

Dread swelled like a pit in his stomach until he felt physically sick. How long had it been since something, anything, mattered so much to him? A very long time, that was for sure.

He was silent the entire drive to her house while she chatted away about... what? Plans? Killers. Magic. He couldn't focus. The fear was all encompassing, which was dumb. He was a warrior.

Inside, Emory tossed her keys on the hall table. "Want a drink? I've got beer in the fridge. Tea? How about wine?"

"Emory, we need to talk."

She froze, her face turning into a mask. "I see." The tone was distant, cool. "That never bodes well, does it? I think perhaps we should sit." She led him into the living room and sat on the couch.

She turned on the lamp on the side table and folded her hands primly in her lap. She looked calm and serene, but there was a pinched look about her eyes that gave away the lie. "What do you want to talk about?" she asked as if she were asking what the weather was going to be like tomorrow.

"I'm not what you think I am."

She blinked. The soft glow of the lamp picked out the fiery shades in her hair. "What are you, then? And what does that have to do with anything?"

"Maybe a lot." He clenched his hands, willing her to understand. "I'm old, Emory. Really old."

"So am I," she pointed out. "I'm a witch, remember?"

"I'm older. A lot older."

She frowned. "How old exactly?"

He took a deep breath. "I am over 10,000 years old. I saw the city of Atlantis fall. I watched the birth of ancient Egypt." He blurted the final truth. "I am a thaumaturge."

CHAPTER
TWENTY-ONE

"Excuse me?" She couldn't have heard him right. Noah was a thaumaturge? How the heck had she missed that? And why hadn't he told her before now?

If portal witches were rare, thaumaturges were extinct, or so she'd thought. They were exceedingly powerful sorcerers. Merlin had been a thaumaturge. According to official witch history, the last one had died over a thousand years ago. Yet here was Noah, claiming to be one.

"I should have told you sooner, but the reason I came here was to say goodbye to Veri before moving on. A person can only live in one place so long before questions are asked. Then I met you, and everything changed. I didn't want to leave anymore. I wanted—"

She held up a hand. "Stop. I need to think."

She realized then she hadn't missed it. She'd suspected, she'd seen the signs, but she'd ignored them because she hadn't wanted to know. Pushed the knowledge away, telling herself she was silly.

Memories flooded her mind: the mention of his family being warriors—a strange term to use if they'd simply served in the army. The Polynesian food that wasn't quite Polynesian, but somehow magical. The restaurant that was partly in Fairy that no one else seemed to know about. Him knowing about Edwina and her abilities without being told. It had been there in front of her the whole time. All the lied and half-truths. She just hadn't wanted to see it.

"Get out," she whispered.

His eyes widened a fraction. "Emory—"

"I can't deal with this right now. Get out."

He nodded, white lines bracketing his mouth. He looked a little gray as he turned and left. She heard the door shut behind him, but it was distant, like it was happening to someone else. She was…what? Angry? Numb? Sad? All those things.

At some point Fred appeared and climbed up to curl around her neck. She stroked his fuzzy butt, the feel of his fluff comforting.

She had no idea how much time had passed when she heard the front door open. Lene sat beside her on the couch. Warm hands wrapped around her cold ones.

"Why exactly did you throw out the best thing that ever happened to you?" she asked without censure.

"He's a thaumaturge and didn't tell me. He lied to me."

"No he didn't. He just didn't tell you everything."

"He should have. He should have trusted me."

"Because you've trusted him with so much, right?"

That hurt. Lene was right, though. She hadn't told him everything. There were still parts of her he didn't know.

"He should have told me before we, um, slept together," she finished lamely.

"I'll give you that, but I don't see what the big deal is."

"He's a freaking sorcerer," Emory said explosively. "And an old one. Like really, really freaking old."

"So? It's not like he eats human flesh." Lene frowned. "Or does he? Better double check with Veri."

"Don't be an idiot."

"Pot, meet kettle. You're the one making a mountain out of a molehill. Since when has age ever mattered to you? You're, what, ninety-three?"

"Ninety-four."

"And how old was the last guy you dated?"

Emory blushed. "Twenty-eight."

"That goes way beyond cougar. Did you tell the young stud how old you were? *What* you were?"

"Of course not. He was a mundane and not from Deepwood. You know that."

Lene leaned back, a smug look on her face. "My point exactly."

"But I'm not a mundane. I can handle the truth."

"Yes, because you're doing so well now."

Lene was right. She was not handling this well at all. She was angry at Noah for lying to her. No, she was hurt he hadn't trusted her with the truth. She was pissed he hadn't told her before they'd gotten intimate. But did it really matter?

All the times she'd said something bad about male magic users popped up in her mind. She'd made it clear she didn't totally trust them. Even if Noah had wanted to tell her the truth, she'd told him she didn't like his kind. Maybe it was as much her fault as it was his.

"I'm confused," she said and moaned.

175

"Of course you are," Lene said, patting her hand. "Because you overthink things. So I'm going to do the thinking for you tonight, okay?"

"Okay."

Lene dragged Emory to the kitchen, Fred still curled around her neck. "You're going to have some tea and go to bed. Once you've had a good night's sleep, you can ponder the implications of not having Noah in your life. Then you can decide what you want to do from there. Sound good?"

"Yeah, except I'm supposed to go with him to question the receptionist at the clinic tomorrow, and. I don't think I'm ready to see him yet."

"Suck it up, sister. You made your bed. You can lie in it and imagine what it would feel like permanently empty."

She didn't have to imagine it. Until Noah, her bed had been empty for a long time. "Fine. Whatever." Now she sounded like Mia.

"The two of you are going have to figure out a way to work together until you decide what you want to do."

This was going to be awkward.

"You told her?" Veri all but shrieked.

Noah winced. "Of course. I couldn't keep lying to her."

"Of course you could have." She paced back and forth in front of her TV. "The less she knows, the better. I *told* you not to say anything. The woman distrusts men with powers. She's going to kill me."

"No she isn't. You're coven."

"How are we going to get you out of this mess?" she said as if he hadn't spoken. "Flowers. Lots and lots of flowers." She whirled and pointed at him. "And chocolate."

"You honestly think Emory is going to forgive me for lying to her because I bring her flowers and chocolates?"

Veri stopped to stare at him. "You're right. Diamonds are better."

"I apologized. She either accepts it or she doesn't." He feared it would be the later. His stomach had been in knots since Emory had thrown him out.

"Goddess, men are idiots," Veri snapped. "You don't understand women at all."

"And you don't understand Emory. Bribes aren't going to fix anything."

"You're right. Throw yourself on her mercy."

"We were supposed to meet in the morning, but she'll probably want to hit the clinic with Edwina or something."

Veri snorted. "Don't give her an option. Stick to your guns. Make her work with you."

"You think forcing Emory to work with me is going to change things?"

His cousin smiled slyly. "Oh, yes."

The clinic opened before Healing Herbs, so Noah picked Emory up early, as planned. She gave him a long look before stepping out her door and locking it behind her. He almost let out a sigh of relief. He hadn't been sure she'd come with him.

The whole drive over, she was silent and so was he. He had no idea what to say. He'd already apologized. What else could he do?

As they entered the clinic, the twenty-something receptionist looked up from her computer screen with an

177

unnaturally wide smile for so early in the morning. Her mousy brown hair, inexpertly streaked with blonde highlights, was done up in a perky ponytail. Her cardigan was a shockingly ugly shade of lime green. Her glasses were more librarian than hipster, and her makeup was reminiscent of the '80s. She looked like a wallflower trying to get noticed.

"Good morning," she said perkily, scanning Noah with blatant appreciation. "Do you have an appointment?"

"No," Emory said with a fake smile. "We're interested in the services the clinic provides. Can I ask you some questions, Miss...?"

"Brooke. Call me Brooke. Everyone does." Her eyes slid to Noah again, and she blushed.

"Okay, Brooke. We're here to talk to you."

"Me? I'm sorry. I don't—"

"This is going to sound silly," Emory said, interrupting her. "But my aunt is a patient here, and she says she gets this tea. It's really unusual. I was wondering what it was? It comes in a red tin."

"Oh, that! Do you want some? It's delish." Brooke jumped out of her chair and crossed the room to a tea and coffee station. She took something off the credenza and waggled it in the air. It was a red tea tin identical to the one Emory had found in Zach's apartment. Brooke returned and handed her the tin. "One of the docs orders it in special. It's some kind of blend that's supposed to boost immunity and brain function, and I don't know what all."

"Do you know where the doctor gets it?"

She shrugged. "Some tea shop. I don't know."

"And this is available to all the patients? Just sitting out?"

"Yeah, of course. Why?" A look of suspicion crossed her face.

"We're here to talk to you about some patients at the clinic," Noah said, glowering at her. He was in full intimidation mode. Emory elbowed him in the ribs and gave him a look she hoped he'd interpret as "chill."

Brooke jumped a little, as if she'd forgotten he was there. "I'm sorry, I can't talk to you about patients. HIPPA rules and everything." She gave Emory an innocent look which didn't fool her one minute. The girl was clearly on guard. She was certain Brooke knew something about the tea and the dead patients.

"Tell me, Brooke, do you know Gary Poe?" Emory asked.

Brooke paled but pulled her shoulders back, tilted her chin up, and glared at them. "I don't know what you're talking about."

"How about Mitch Kerrigan? Zach Polinsky? They were patients here. You know they're all dead, right?"

Brooke was turning green. "You're lying," she whispered.

"Listen, little girl," Noah snarled, stepping into her personal space, his warrior routine in full swing. She looked like she might faint on the spot. "You will stop lying and speak the truth." His words were a thinly veiled threat and something more. Power shimmered through the air.

"Or what?" Brooke tried to look defiant but only managed to look pathetic.

There was a pause. "Or I will make sure the authorities know you're responsible for the deaths of these three men."

"But I'm not," she wailed.

"Brooke? Everything okay?" A middle-aged man with a receding hairline and a well-trimmed salt-and-pepper goatee poked his head out of one of the offices.

"Fine, Doc. Everything's fine."

The doctor retreated into his office, slamming the door. Apparently saving his receptionist wasn't worth standing up to Noah. Emory didn't blame him. Noah was pretty intimidating when he wanted to be.

"You better tell us the truth, Brooke," Emory said softly. "I know a lot of very important people who can make sure you get lost down a very dark hole."

"It's not my fault, okay?" she whimpered.

"Then whose fault is it?"

She closed her eyes and sucked in a deep breath. "My boyfriend, okay?"

"What does he have to do with this?" Noah demanded.

"He asked me to keep an eye out for certain kinds of patients."

"What kind of patients?" Emory prodded.

Brooke fidgeted, hesitating.

"Brooke," Noah warned.

"Patients who were highly stressed. Not sleeping. That sort of thing. But were otherwise healthy. Patients with a certain amount of money."

"These people weren't rich," Emory pointed out.

"Not rich," Brook admitted. "But with easily accessible income. Savings. Regular Social Security checks. That kind of stuff."

Gary and Mitch might have fit that bill—she remembered seeing healthy bank balances on Gary's statements and Mitch clearly had some source of income—but Zach certainly hadn't. "What did you do with those patients?"

Brooke sighed. "I was to make sure they drank some of the tea. Not the stuff out here, but this." She reached under her desk and brought out a tin identical to the one on the tea and coffee service.

Emory took it from her and removed the lid. Faint symbols shimmered above it.

"It's not the same," she told Noah. "Similar, but not quite. This stuff's been bespelled."

Brooke frowned. "What are you talking about?"

"Never mind. What were you to do after you gave the patient the tea?"

"Give them my boyfriend's card." She dug around in her purse and handed Emory a business card. It was simple, white, with only a phone number. "Once they drank the tea, I gave them the card and told them if they called, they'd find way more help than they'd ever get here."

"And Gary, Mitch, and Zach were the people you gave the card to?"

"Among others."

Noah and Emory exchanged glances.

"I want their names, Brooke."

"I can't—"

Noah didn't say a word, but his expression spoke volumes. She picked up a pen and started writing. After a minute she handed Emory the list.

"Thank you." Emory started to turn but stopped. "Why Zach? He didn't have any money." Unlike the other two, he'd lived in a cheap rental and drove a car that was falling apart.

"But he did. I mean, he talked about it all the time. How he'd bought a flat-screen TV or a new car or whatever."

Zach had lied to impress the young receptionist. "Brooke, if you call your boyfriend and tell him anything, anything at all, I will find you. Understand?"

She shook like a leaf. Tears welled in her eyes. "I won't say anything, I promise."

Noah drove while Emory researched the names on her smartphone. She wanted to avoid talking to him as long as possible. She just couldn't deal with personal stuff at the moment. She needed to focus on the investigation.

What she found was shocking.

"Every single one of these people, except for the three we already knew about, has recently been in the news," she told him.

"For what?"

"Going stark raving nuts. One of them is the guy who attacked me and that jogger in the park. Another is the woman from the mall. There are half a dozen others who have had psychotic breaks. All of them are locked up in the psych wards in local hospitals."

"This can't be a coincidence."

She frowned at the list. "The only three who are dead are the three we found."

"The three that were definitely supernaturals."

She glanced at him, startled. "How could you know that?" She certainly hadn't been able to tell.

He shrugged. "We already figured Gary Poe had some connection to the supernatural community since he came to you for help, right? And Mitch...I always suspected something about him. So I did some digging last night. Looks like all three had limited supernatural abilities."

She squirmed at the thought of what they could have been doing last night. "Like what?"

He kept his eyes glued to the road. "Poe was part Sidhe. Not a lot but enough to make a difference. I am not sure how his abilities manifested, but he definitely had something. My buddy Mitch was part djinn. He couldn't shift, but he was unusually strong and fast. Enough to tip the scales, not enough to alert the wrong people, which explains some things I saw in the Gulf."

"And Zach?"

"Witchblood, like us. No abilities."

"Oh dear."

"You think that means something?"

"Hard to tell unless we know if the others who didn't die were supernatural or human. It might make a creepy sort of sense, though. Maybe the spell, whatever it was for, affected humans and supernaturals in different ways. It made the humans crazy, but it was deadly for supernaturals."

"Sea gods, that's messed up. Have you figured out what the spell is for yet?"

"I did a little research last night. It seems to be sort of a hypnotic thing. It opens the ensorcelled to suggestion. That's probably how Brooke got them to call a strange number and seek out additional help when they were already getting help at the clinic."

"But you don't think she bespelled the tea herself."

She shook her head. "Pretty sure she's human. Wouldn't have the skill set."

"It's similar to the deadly spell, but not the same."

"And it's not nearly as strong either. My guess is this spell was meant to soften them up while the second spell, administered through another dose of the tea, was to finish them off. Figuratively speaking, of course. I don't think death was the ultimate goal. I think Brooke's boyfriend had a different end game in mind."

"Like what?"

She gazed out the window at the passing scenery. "That is the question, isn't it?"

"We might need backup on this."

"We should call Edwina."

He shot her a look. "Edwina?"

"You'd be surprised at her skill set."

He placed the call while she stared out the window as if none of it mattered. But her stomach was twisted in knots. At some point they were going to have to talk, hash things out one way or the other. She wasn't looking forward to it.

CHAPTER
TWENTY-TWO

Lewis Binder, Brooke's boyfriend, lived in a nice cookie-cutter home in one of those housing developments that was no more than five years old, with houses costing no less than half a million dollars. In Deepwood—heck, just about anywhere—that was a very nice house.

"That's a large place for one guy," Noah said as he parked across the street.

It had to be five bedrooms at least. The yard was enormous and probably needed a multitude of gardeners to keep it looking perfectly manicured.

"I wonder what Binder does for a living that he can afford this?" Noah mused.

"Nothing good, I'll bet. Not if he's spellcasting people to death," Emory said grimly.

A vintage VW Van in lemon yellow pulled up behind them, and Edwina climbed out. She wore a blue and white striped sundress, a floppy straw hat, and her ever present Doc Martens. Emory was suddenly shaky. Go time. Wasn't that what they said in the movies?

They climbed out of their respective cars. As if on cue, everyone turned toward Binder's house.

As they approached on foot, she saw the faint shimmer of wards at every door and window. "He's very security conscious," Emory murmured. "He's warded it like crazy."

"I can't see anything," Noah said, squinting against the glare of the morning sun.

"Nor can I," Edwina agreed.

"You wouldn't," she said. "I doubt anyone but a spellwalker could. My little gift, remember?"

"Can you get through?" Edwina asked.

She grinned, though it was forced. "Does a unicorn fart in the woods?"

"I don't know," Noah said. "Never met one."

She gritted her teeth, determined to ignore him. As they drew even with the wards, she reached out and mentally tweaked the spell. It was ridiculously easy. Once finished she could pass through without a tickle.

"I'll go around back," Edwina said and slipped away before Emory could protest. Not that she would have. Despite the tension between them, she'd rather be close to Noah than not. Something to ponder later.

He rang the doorbell, and they waited, Emory trying desperately not to fidget. The tension between them was palpable.

"Maybe he's not home," he suggested.

"Oh, he's home," she assured him. "I can sense him through the wards."

"He's a witch?"

She snorted. "Warlock. Witches don't kill people. At least I think he's a warlock. I guess he could have had someone set up the wards."

He rang again, this time leaning on the bell for a good thirty seconds. After what seemed an eternity, the door swung open. The guy standing there was skinny, pale, and wearing a perfectly pressed black suit. An expensive suit, with matching black shirt, tie, and shoes. The color did not flatter his pasty complexion.

"Lewis Binder?" Emory asked.

Binder looked from her to Noah, and then slammed the door in their faces. She could hear footsteps pounding across marble. Noah kicked the door open, and they gave chase. Well, Noah gave chase. Emory sort of panted along behind. Her flip-flops were not made for running.

They ran through the cavernous marble entryway, past an office that looked oddly like a doctor's office, and into an enormous living area in time to see Lewis slip out the sliding glass doors to the backyard. Lewis took off, running hell bent for leather, Noah hot on his tail.

Halfway across the lawn, Edwina stepped out from behind a bush, clotheslining Binder like a pro-wrestler. He flipped under her arm and hit the ground hard. He lay flat on his back, gasping for air. Poor Lewis hadn't had a snowball's chance.

Noah grabbed Lewis by the collar and yanked him to his feet. He gave him a good shake, and when Binder tried to squirm away, punched him in the face. He dropped like a stone.

"What'd you do that for?" Edwina grumbled. "I had him right where I wanted him."

"We do not have time to mess around. He could have ensorcelled other people. They could be in danger. We need to know why." Noah was practically snarling.

Edwina gave him a look that would have withered a normal man. "And punching him unconscious is going to help that how?"

"I might have hit him harder than I meant, but he'll be fine."

"Would you two stop arguing and bring him inside? We do not have time for this."

Noah sighed. "Yes, ma'am." He slung Binder over his shoulder like a sack of potatoes. Inside, he tossed him on the couch while Edwina slumped in a chair across the room. Emory grabbed a glass from the kitchen and filled it with ice water. As she did, she noticed a familiar tin sitting on the counter. She grabbed it.

Stomping back into the living room, she flung the water in Binder's face. He came awake instantly, spluttering and cursing like a sailor.

"Welcome back, Mr. Binder. I think it's time you answered a few questions." Emory crossed her arms and slapped on her witchiest glare. The kind that said, "I'll turn you into a toad if you don't cooperate."

Binder spluttered a bit, wiping water from his eyes. "How dare you?" He tried to sound outraged, but it came across more scared than anything.

Noah loomed over the cowering Binder. "Listen, you worm. You will answer this woman's questions, or I will have your spleen for dinner."

"You wouldn't dare," he whispered.

"Try me," Noah said grimly. "You know what I am, do you not?"

Lewis Binder paled. "You're FBI."

The three of them gave each other confused looks. Emory supposed that with his dark cargo pants and tinted sunglasses, Noah did look somewhat *Men in Black*. There was probably some law against impersonating a federal agent, but they were dealing with seriously nasty magic here, and he'd been in the military, after all.

Noah gave Binder a smile that spoke of death and darker things. He cowered against the sofa cushions.

"Fine." Binder pouted. "What do you want to know?"

"I want to know why you killed three people," Emory said.

"I don't know what you're talking about." He went ghost white and beads of sweat popped out across his forehead.

"Really?" she snapped. "Then maybe we should make you drink some of this." She waved the tin of tea she'd found in his kitchen in front of his face.

He swallowed hard. "N-no. Please don't."

"Then let's start with why you killed those people."

"That wasn't supposed to happen." Lewis was shaking.

"What was supposed to happen?" Edwina drawled. She'd propped her feet on the coffee table, her boots scuffing the ebony wood.

"Money, you know," Binder said. "I was supposed to get money."

"All right, why did you bespell the tea?" Emory demanded

"But I didn't," he whined. "I don't even know how to bespell tea. Or anything else, for that matter. My partner did it."

Partner? She sighed and pinched the bridge of her nose. "Start from the beginning."

He sighed. "I'm a financial planner, okay?"

Noah and Emory exchanged glances. The office they'd seen at the front of his fancy-pants house wasn't set up like a financial planner's. It was set up like a doctor's office, with diagrams of the human body and lists of herbs and their health benefits. "Go on," she prompted.

"Things weren't going well. For years I struggled to get clients. Then I met this guy, right? He told me, for a percentage of the profits, he could get people to invest with me. Lots of people."

Emory snorted. "Let me guess. He told you he could do it with magic, and you bought that?"

"I dated this girl in college. She could do stuff. Real magic stuff, like light candles with her mind. I figured what the heck? Give it a try. So I agreed to a small spell to attract more clients. Easy. Nothing dark or horrible."

"What spell did he use?" Emory asked.

Binder shook his head. "Don't know. He told me it was an attraction spell. Nothing interfering with free will."

Nothing unusual there. She had used the odd attraction spell or two to draw in clients, among other things. Especially in the early days when customers had been few and money tight. "Then what?"

"I got more clients and started making money. Some of these people were loaded. I was making a real living, a life I'd never imagined. I bought this house." He waved his arms. "Began living like I'd always wanted." He winced. "But then I gave somebody bad advice, and he lost money—a lot of it. And he wanted it back."

"He threatened to turn you in to the cops?" Edwina asked.

"Worse." Binder looked positively green. "He threatened to turn his 'associates' loose on me."

"That doesn't sound good," Noah said blandly.

"It wasn't," Lewis admitted. "I'm pretty sure he's connected. Like with the mob or something."

"What did you do?" Emory asked.

"I didn't know what to do. I needed more money. I asked my partner for a stronger attraction spell to get more clients, but it wasn't happening fast enough."

"So you decided to try something else," she guessed.

"My partner told me he could cast a spell that would make people just hand over their money. You know, like a donation."

Emory barely refrained from an eye roll. "And you roped in your girlfriend."

Binder fidgeted. "It seemed harmless. Brooke works at this natural health clinic. I figured people who use those places usually have more than enough to be comfortable. I figured I could have her identify people who didn't have families or anyone to worry about them or their bank accounts. Send them to me, then I could use the spell on them."

"That's what the tea at the clinic was for. To make them susceptible to her suggestion to call you." That wasn't how magic was supposed to work.

He nodded. "Once I got them to come in, I posed as a natural healer and gave them tea. Told them it was to reduce stress and enhance their natural ability to attract, well, whatever it was they were looking for. Women, money, inner peace. Once the spell took hold, they were basically in a trance."

"And then what?"

"I'd have them write me a very generous check as a 'consultant's fee' and send them on their way with orders they were not to question the payment and to forget all about me."

"Fast, easy money," Edwina said dryly. "What went wrong?"

"I don't know!" Binder wailed as if he were somehow the victim. "At first everything went fine, but the suggestion didn't take with this one woman. I guess the spell wasn't strong enough, or she didn't drink enough tea. She returned, demanding her money back, threatening to call the cops. I asked my partner for a new spell, something a lot stronger. Everything went back to normal. I gave people the stronger tea, just in case. Then I saw on the news that one of my clients had gone crazy and attacked a woman in the park."

Holy cannoli, the guy she'd run into. The one who'd attacked the jogger.

"Then more were in the news, going crazy. Eventually the effects wore off, but it turned them psychotic for a while. I thought everything was fine. I had no idea anyone had died. Honestly."

"Didn't you try to get hold of your partner?" Emory asked.

"Of course I did." He looked like he was about to faint. "But he wouldn't pick up the phone, and I don't know where he lives. I don't even know his real name. He told me to call him Mr. Black."

How original. "And your clients? You didn't let a few crazy people stop you, did you?"

"No," he admitted. "I needed the money. How am I supposed to live?"

"At least you get to," Noah murmured. A muscle in his jaw flexed.

"And so innocent people died to feed your greed." Emory shook her head. "But why Zach Polinsky? He wasn't wealthy or even comfortable. He was barely making it paycheck to paycheck."

"That was a mistake. He was bragging to Brooke about all this stuff he owned. She thought he was loaded. Stupid woman." He glanced at Noah's stony expression. "I didn't take anything from him, I swear. When I realized how broke he was, I gave him the tea and told him it would help him attract more attention from the ladies. He drank it, and I sent him home, told him to forget about me. I figured everything was fine."

"But he stole the tea," Emory guessed, remembering the tin she'd found at his place. "He probably thought if one dose would attract women, several doses would attract even more. Instead it killed him."

"What's going to happen to me?" Binder was practically whimpering.

Noah made a nasty sound. "Deep, dark hole, I imagine."

"After the witch council gets done with you," Edwina agreed.

"The what?" Binder looked like he might pass out. Good. He deserved the worst they'd do to him.

Edwina pulled out her phone and dialed a number. "We found the killer."

CHAPTER
TWENTY-THREE

Someone from the witch council arrived soon after to take charge of Lewis Binder. Emory had no idea what they planned to do with him, but hopefully they'd dump him where he'd never see sunlight again. Maybe he hadn't meant to kill anybody but using magic in such an irresponsible way was dangerous beyond belief.

According to Lewis Binder, Brooke had had no idea what he and his partner were doing. "Don't worry," Edwina assured Emory. "I'm going to pay her a little visit. Put her on the straight and narrow."

"Hopefully for the rest of her life."

But there was still the matter of Lewis's partner. "How are we going to find him?" Emory wondered aloud.

"Is there some witchy thing you can do?" Noah asked.

She considered that a moment. It was difficult to think with him so near and things still unresolved between them. "I might be able to use the partner's spell to put a back trace on him. Sort of like putting a trace on a cellphone. I'll need the whole coven, though. That sort of thing takes a lot of power."

He nodded. "You should do it. We need to stop this guy."

"Listen, Noah..."

He turned to look at her, and her heart started thudding so hard, she could hear it in her ears, feel it fluttering in her throat. "Um...." She was unsure what to say.

"Just say it," Noah said stiffly, his eyes never leaving hers. She couldn't read his expression at all.

He wasn't going to make this easy for her. Fair enough.

"Noah, I am really, really sorry about how I reacted. I just...it was such a surprise." That was an understatement. "And I guess—" She paused. "I was upset you hadn't trusted me enough to tell me the truth earlier. I know that's silly, because we don't know each other, but... it hurt, and I lashed out. For that I'm really sorry."

He nodded, shoving his hands in his pockets. "I get that. It's a lot to take in."

"I care about you. I know it hasn't been very long—"

He grabbed her hands. "I care about you, too, Emory."

"You do?"

He smiled. "More than you can imagine. Think you can deal with me being a thaumaturge? I'm not like him, you know. The one who hurt your mom."

"I know you aren't. And yeah"—she grinned— "pretty sure I can deal."

When they finally came up for air, she was grinning like an idiot.

"Now," Noah said at last, "let's go catch a bad guy."

Emory poured the bespelled tea leaves into a small copper bowl, then placed the bowl on a brazier in the middle of the circle. Around her she heard the chants of her sister witches and Noah's deeper tones. While Edwina wasn't witchblood, and Noah was something else entirely, they were still supernatural and powerful, and would be enough to hold the corners while Emory, Lene, and Veri did the heavy lifting.

She poured purified water into the bowl until the leaves were covered. Under it coals glowed like red eyes. Moving her hand slowly over the bowl in a clockwise motion, she murmured the words of the spell that would activate a trace on whoever had ensorcelled the tea. The ancient language of the portal witches tripped off her tongue, and she could see the symbols of her spell fall from her lips to the bowl, mixing with the tea leaves and water.

The water swirled faster and faster, a vortex of power twisting down into the mixture. Then it went flat and still as a pond on a summer's day. The water shimmered, turned black, then clear as crystal. A face appeared.

"Holy freaking Hades. I know who Binder's partner is."

If life were an episode of *Cops,* or Deepwood Police Chief Nathan Dekes had been Lt. Joe Kenda, the street would have been crammed with black-and-whites, unmarked police vehicles, and swirling blue and red lights. But it was quiet except for a barking dog.

A black SUV with tinted windows slid to a stop at the curb while Emory and Noah watched from his jeep across the street. Two more SUVs joined the first. The witch council representative—Emory never did get his name and wasn't sure she wanted to—got out of the first vehicle and strode to the front door of the Craftsman cottage while his men ranged out around the house to prevent escape. She half expected the neighbors to pop up to express curiosity, but the houses remained dark and silent, as if everyone knew something big was going down, and they had no interest in being part of it.

The councilman rapped on the front door once, twice. On the third knock, the porch light flipped on. The front door swung open, and a man stood there in his boxers, beer belly sagging over a stretched-out elastic waistband. It was not a pretty sight.

Emory rolled down her window so she could hear better. The voices were low but carried easily through the darkness.

"Whaddaya want?" the man snarled.

The councilman flashed his badge. "Witch council. Come with me, sir."

The man crossed his arms. "Screw that." He didn't ask what the witch council was or question the credentials. He didn't even seem surprised to him.

"Sir, you will come with me willingly, or I will make you come with me."

A sly look spread over the man's face. "Fine. Make me."

The councilman stepped back and waved to an agent who was standing just out of sight. The agent stepped up and waved one hand. It wasn't dramatic or anything, but the results were. The boxer-wearing jerk dropped like a stone.

Agents swarmed in, slapped cuffs on his wrists, and hauled him to one of the SUVs.

A woman appeared in the doorway. "My husband! Stop. Where are you taking him? What's going on?"

She caught sight of the jeep and Emory. Wearing nothing but a thin robe and slippers, the woman stormed across the road. Emory recognized her immediately.

"Holy cannoli," she muttered.

"What?" Noah asked, but there was no time to explain.

"You did this," Susan snarled in Emory's face. "Why? Because I wouldn't leave him? You had no right. No right!"

"You came to me for help, remember? It was your choice until we found out he was killing people. Then it became *our* business."

Susan snorted. No longer the proper church woman, she looked like a wild thing, rage twisting her features into a caricature. "You lying snake. He would never——"

"Ma'am, please step away from the jeep and stop verbally abusing my partner," Noah said.

"Or what, you big bully?"

"Or I will have to restrain you."

"Go ahead and try," Susan screamed, "you devil worshipping heathen. You witch! You——" She reached in and slapped Emory across the face before Emory had time to react.

Noah was out of the jeep in a second, grabbing Susan and wrenching her arms behind her back. One of the agents from the witch council jogged over to take her into custody, handing her off to the man who'd downed Susan's husband.

"Thanks for your help, guys. I couldn't have done this without you," the lead agent said, offering them a tired smile. "We're stretched pretty thin at the moment." He scraped a hand through his hair. "We really need to read Chief Dekes in."

Emory wondered how Nathan Dekes would feel about that. "What's going to happen to Susan?"

"We'll interrogate her, see what she knows. If she was in on her husband's little money-making plot, she'll pay just like he will. If not, we'll 'correct' her memories and send her home."

Correct. There was a euphemism if ever she'd heard one. She stared at the SUV that held her former customer. "If she is innocent, give her some nice memories, okay? She's suffered enough."

"Will do. You kids go home and get some rest. You look as tired as I feel." The man from the witch council turned on his heel and strode to his SUV. The three vehicles pulled out and took off, their taillights disappearing around the corner.

"We're not going to tell them about the people we buried in the bayou?" she asked.

Noah shook his head. "Better they rest in peace. I know Mitch would appreciate it."

Probably Gary Poe, too. It had been a lovely spot, and she could visit them on Samhain, plant some birdfoot violets. Make sure their spirits rested in peace.

She let out a jaw-cracking yawn. "I could definitely crawl into bed right now."

Noah gave her a wicked grin. "So could I."

She had the distinct feeling he didn't mean to sleep.

"You're telling me this crazy Susan chick's husband was behind all this?" Veri asked the next day as the three witches gathered around a box of Virgil's donuts set out on the counter of Healing Herbs.

"Yes," Emory confirmed as she polished off a coconut crème filled donut dusted with lime sugar. "Susan's husband, who went around calling himself Mr. Black, is a low-level warlock. He knows enough dark magic he was able to put a spell on the tea he had his partner, Binder, use to bespell unwitting victims. They'd fork over a ton of cash and the two would split it. Simple greed."

"Simple my ample backside," Lene said. "People *died*. That poor Mr. Poe. I'll never forget. Not to mention Noah's friend and that poor kid."

Emory agreed. "At least we were able to stop Binder and Black. They'll never hurt anyone else."

"What about Susan?" Lene asked. "Was she involved?"

"Not at first. In fact, she really did want to stop his abuse," Emory explained. "Then she discovered his secret stash of cash and, once she figured out his game, she wanted in. She figured she could take the money and run. Which was why she was trying to protect him."

"He was her golden gander," Veri mused.

"In a manner of speaking," Emory said. "But thanks to Edwina and Noah, they're behind bars where they belong and the money that was left has been returned to its owners."

"And how about our new witch?" Veri asked. "How's she coming along?"

Emory sighed. "Mia is going to take a little time. But she'll get there." At least she hoped so.

"Speaking of Noah..." Lene switched subjects with a smirk.

"Were we?" Emory asked innocently.

"Spill," Veri ordered. "I know you two are an item."

"Yes! Spill!" Lene demanded.

Emory felt herself blush as she faced Veri. "You're not mad?"

"Girl, why would I be mad? I'm beyond thrilled. My favorite cousin and my BFF? I expect to be named witchmother of your firstborn."

Emory snorted. "I think you're getting ahead of yourself, Veri."

Veri flicked a lock of hair behind her shoulder. "Nonsense. I've seen it in the cards."

Emory eyed her friend warily. "Seen what exactly?"

Veri's grin widened. "You'll see."

THE END

WISTERIA, WITCHERY, AND WOE
the second book in the
Deepwood Witches Mysteries
Coming soon.

A Note From Shéa MacLeod

Thank you for reading. If you enjoyed this book, I'd appreciate it if you'd help others find it so they can enjoy it too.

Please return to the site where you purchased this book and leave a review to let other potential readers know what you liked or didn't like about the story.

Book updates can be found at www.sheamacleod.com

Be sure to sign up for my mailing list so you don't miss out!
https://www.subscribepage.com/cozymystery

You can follow me on Facebook
https://www.facebook.com/sheamacleodcozymysteries/ or on Instagram under **@SheaMacLeod_Author**.

About Shéa MacLeod

Shéa MacLeod is the author of the *Lady Rample Mysteries*, the popular historical cozy mystery series set in 1930s London. She's also written paranormal romance, paranormal mysteries, urban fantasy, and contemporary romances with a splash of humor. She resides in the leafy green hills outside Portland, Oregon, where she indulges her fondness for strong coffee, Ancient Aliens reruns, lemon curd, and dragons.

Because everything's better with dragons.

Potions, Poisons and Peril

Other Cozy Mysteries by Shéa MacLeod

Deepwood Witches Mysteries
Potions, Poisons, and Peril
Wisteria, Witchery, and Woe
Moonlight, Magic, and Murder
Dreams Divination, and Danger

Viola Roberts Cozy Mysteries
The Corpse in the Cabana
The Stiff in the Study
The Poison in the Pudding
The Body in the Bathtub
The Venom in the Valentine
The Remains in the Rectory
The Death in the Drink

Lady Rample Mysteries
Lady Rample Steps Out
Lady Rample Spies a Clue
Lady Rample and the Silver Screen
Lady Rample Sits In
Lady Rample and the Ghost of Christmas Past
Lady Rample and Cupid's Kiss
Lady Rample and the Mysterious Mr. Singh

Sugar Martin Vintage Cozy Mysteries
A Death in Devon
A Grave Gala

Non-Cozy Mysteries by Shéa MacLeod

Intergalactic Investigations (SciFi Mysteries)
Infinite Justice
A Rage of Angels

Other Books by Shéa MacLeod

Notting Hill Diaries
To Kiss a Prince
Kissing Frogs
Kiss Me, Chloe
Kiss Me, Stupid
Kissing Mr. Darcy

Cupcake Goddess Novelettes
Be Careful What You Wish For
Nothing Tastes As Good
Soulfully Sweet
A Stich in Time

Sunwalker Saga
Kissed by Blood
Kissed by Darkness
Kissed by Fire
Kissed by Smoke
Kissed by Moonlight
Kissed by Ice
Kissed by Eternity
Kissed by Destiny

Sunwalker Saga: Soulshifter Trilogy
Fearless
Haunted
Soulshifter

Dragon Wars
Dragon Warrior
Dragon Lord
Dragon Goddess
Green Witch
Dragon Corps
Dragon's Angel
Dragon Mage

Made in the USA
Monee, IL
09 October 2020